PIPERS GAP

PIPERS GAP

C. David Gelly

Palmetto Publishing Group
Charleston, SC

Pipers Gap
Copyright © 2018 by C. David Gelly
All rights reserved

First Edition

Printed in the United States

ISBN-13: 978-1-64111-209-3
ISBN-10: 1-64111-209-3

LULU . . . YOU ARE MY . . . JOIE DE VIVRE . . .

Art, freedom, and creativity will change society faster than politics.

. . .Victor Pinchuk

ACKNOWLEDGMENTS

To all of you who have read and enjoyed *Fancy Gap, Orchard Gap,* and Volunteer Gap, my thanks for your support and encouragement! *Pipers Gap* is the fourth novel in the Gap series. While it is not necessary to read the prior three novels in the series, it is recommended that you do to gain greater understanding of the main characters.

If you enjoy my work, please tell all your friends and family. Post great reviews on Amazon, and post shout-outs about this novel and all my novels on Facebook, Instagram, Twitter, Pinterest, and so forth. I write . . . you read . . . and spread the good news!

Keep the faith as you journey to Pipers Gap . . . and back!

Bad politicians are sent to Washington by good people who don't vote.

—*William E. Simon*

CHAPTER 1

SHERIFF LEROY JEFFERSON HAD JUST FINISHED HIS Monday morning staff briefing. He was pleased that the past weekend had been relatively peaceful in Carroll County, Virginia. No one had killed themselves or anyone else, and only a few of the local denizens had been arrested for drunk driving.

He left the staff room and walked back to his office. On his way, he stopped at the coffee pot and poured more coffee into his cup. He was still tired from the weekend chores he had to take care of on his farm. He was blessed to have a working farm on the land he so loved.

Levi Blackburn, his most senior detective, came up behind him. "Now, Leroy, I must say you seemed to be a bit stiff today, old man. Has your lovely wife, Laneisha, been having her way with you on the weekend?"

Leroy smiled. "Levi, I can till the land and bail hay as well as any man and bring a smile to my wife's pretty face and still have more in the tank than you ever will!"

They both erupted in laughter and did not see Leroy's secretary approach.

"Sheriff, if you can stop giggling anytime this morning, our favorite UPS driver, George, just dropped this off for you."

The sheriff took the package and looked at Levi.

"You expecting anything from anyone, boss?"

Leroy shook his head from side to side. "No, I'm not, Levi. I don't have a clue."

They both closely examined the small package. It was wrapped in plain brown paper but did not have a return address on it. Leroy took the package into his office. Levi followed.

Leroy put the package to his ear and shook it. He paused and shook it again. "Jeez, Levi, I think there's liquid inside this package. Now you take a listen."

Levi reached over and held the package between two fingers on his right hand. He shook it gently and shook it several more times. "Sure nuff, Sheriff, there is some sort of liquid in there. But I think there's something else."

Leroy sat at his desk and opened the bottom drawer. He reached in and removed a large magnifying glass. He slowly went over every inch of the package.

Levi was getting impatient. "Well, boss, what do you think? Anything look strange or unusual?"

The sheriff handed Levi the package. "Take another look, Levi."

Levi took the magnifying glass and held the package very close as he turned it from side to side. He set the package down on the sheriff's desk and shook his head. "Heck, Leroy, I think we're being a tad bit over-cautious. Let's just open the darn thing and see what's inside. It's too darn small to be a bomb. I'll do it for you if you like."

The sheriff reached into the top drawer of his desk and removed a small knife. He never looked at Levi as he slowly slit down the side of the package from top to bottom. Within a few moments, the outside brown paper covering fell off and onto his desk.

What was left was a small glass cylinder that looked like a small milk bottle and had a screw top. It was completely wrapped in plain white paper. Leroy slowly used his knife to cut a seam along the side of the cylinder. Levi's eyes were glued to what was happening in front of him.

Once Leroy reached the bottom of the cylinder, the inner wrapping came loose. He peeled it off the entire cylinder and set the paper on his desk. Levi could not take his eyes off what was inside the clear glass cylinder. He squinted as he tried to take a closer look.

He slowly unscrewed the top open until it came loose. He quickly tightened it up again, as the stench that seeped out was horrible.

The sheriff slowly unfolded the white paper, as there appeared to be words typed on the inside of the paper. He turned the paper right side up and began to read what was typed: "You motherfuckers might have killed me, but you will feel my wrath from the depths of hell. Tommie Cruz."

At that very moment Levi's hands started to shake as he handed the cylinder to the sheriff.

Leroy looked at him. "What the hell is in there, Levi?"

Levi thought he was going to puke when he blurted out, "Son of a bitch, Leroy. I think it's a . . . *penis!*"

CHAPTER 2

ELENA SOKOLOV OPENED HER EYES AS SHE FELT THE VAN she was in slow down. She looked ahead and saw a large sign that read: "Jackman-Armstrong Maine Border Crossing." The man driving the van, Traktor Berezin, turned the light on in the van.

Natalia Popov, who was sitting next to Elena, woke up and smiled at her. She reached over and took hold of Elena's hand. She was becoming accustomed to the procedure when they encountered customs and border patrol officials.

Their journey had started some weeks earlier in St. Petersburg, Russia. After months of seclusion in a remote area of the city, their training was completed. The seven girls in the van had been trained as a unit. All came from different areas of the vast Russian countryside but were recruited because they were smart and beautiful.

All seven were between the ages of fourteen and fifteen years old. They were physically mature for their age and were tall and leggy. Four were natural blondes, two were brunettes, and one was a redhead. They all had blue eyes.

Their abductions were all well thought out. The Russian mafia left no stone unturned in its clandestine selection process. The girls were abducted and taken to a secret training center. Local police were bribed to not conduct any investigation into the abductions.

Their parents were frustrated, as there was no information as to where their daughters may be. They appeared to have vanished into thin air. Some of the parents had hired private investigators, but that was to no avail, as investigators soon realized that the abductions were orchestrated by the mafia, or the Bratva, as they were known.

Not long after they were assembled in the safe house, the girls were segregated into groups of seven. They were housed in large cabins, where each girl had a small bedroom. They were soon introduced to a man who they would come to know as their father. This person oversaw their training and indoctrination.

The Bratva understood that some of the girls might not like their new lives and might try to escape. Within two days of their arrival, the girls were assembled at twilight outside of their cabins. It was suggested to them in no uncertain terms that if they tried to escape or communicate with others about their new lives, there would be dire consequences.

They were shown pictures of their parents and siblings. Their new father, as the leader of the camp was called, explained that some, if not all, of their parents and siblings would be beaten and killed if they ever spoke of them to others or tried to contact them. Each of the girls shivered, as there was no doubt that their parents would suffer if they didn't embrace their new life.

He let his message sink in before two men appeared with a young girl who looked as though she should be part of their group. She sobbed as she sat in a chair and listened to the father tell the girls that this girl had tried to escape.

He then passed around his iPhone, which showed pictures of the girl's parents. They were slumped over a chair. They had been shot in the head—execution style. The girl in the chair sobbed uncontrollably as each girl looked at the pictures. They cried as well.

The father stood behind the girls and told them that there was a consequence for her actions. He slowly drew his pistol from his jacket and shot the girl in the back of her head. Each of the seven girls clearly understood *the message.*

CHAPTER 3

LOUISA HAWKE POUNDED THE STEERING WHEEL OF HER
Volvo as she drove into the fading sunlight. Tears
streamed down her cheeks as she squinted to see the
road ahead. "I'm such a fucking idiot!" she screamed
time after time into the nothingness of the space around
her. Her throat was irritated. She had been driving for
thirty-six hours straight on her way to California.

She knew she had to rest, as she hadn't eaten for a
day and was famished. Up ahead, she saw an exit ramp
some forty miles outside of a small town she had never
heard of. The light on the Hampton Inn sign came on
as she pulled into the parking lot.

The parking lot was mostly empty as she parked in
a spot nearest the entrance. With Kleenex in hand, she
wiped the last tears from her cheeks and turned off
the ignition with her right hand. Her roller board hit

the ground hard as she yanked it from the back of the Volvo.

The older woman glanced up from behind the front desk as Louisa came through the doors. "Welcome to the Hampton Inn, sweetie," she offered with a smile on her face.

Louisa looked up and offered a tepid smile back at her.

The woman held up her hand. "You're in luck, young lady. We do have a room for you. As a matter of fact, you can choose just about any room you want."

"I only need a nice room with clean sheets and a shower with hot water," Louisa offered as she reached for her credit card. "And I'm mighty hungry too. So, if you can recommend a restaurant I can walk to, that would be appreciated."

The woman glanced at Louisa's credit card. "Well, Louisa, I can't think of any places to eat nearby that you can walk to. Most would require that you drive apiece to get some eats. Now if you don't mind me sayin', you look a bit road weary, young lady, so let me suggest something. We have a real nice kitchen here at the Hampton Inn. Sean, our chef, will be here for another hour, and he can cook up whatever you might desire. And you can sit right at the bar and have a conversation with the bartender, which tonight will be me. Oh, and my name is Hattie Bob."

Louisa drew a brighter smile as she looked at Hattie Bob. "Now that is the best offer I've had all day. I will take you up on that."

"Then skedaddle on up to your room and take that warm shower, change your clothes, and get on back down here for the best meal you will ever have in New Mexico."

Once inside her room, Louisa laid her clothes out on the bed and took the toiletries into the bathroom. She stopped in front of the bathroom mirror and didn't like what she saw. Her eyes were swollen from all her crying. Her hair was a mess, and she reeked of body odor.

She reached into the shower stall, turned the hot water on, and let it get as hot as it could. Once in the middle of the tub, she stood for several minutes as the water cascaded all over her body.

The shampoo spread all over her head as she massaged it into her scalp. With that faint pleasure came a weak smile that barely crossed her cheeks. Her body was soon covered with lather from the soap, which she rubbed vigorously in her hands.

The thought of filling the tub with hot water and lying in it for the rest of the night crossed her mind. Yet the hunger pains that now swirled in her stomach quickly overruled such lounging thoughts.

As she stood naked in front of the mirror blow drying her long, red hair, she forced herself to stand up straight. Her eyes examined every nook and cranny of her own torso. Tears quickly welled up again when she knew that the only eyes she desired to be looking at her body were not there, and it was her fault.

She dressed quickly and headed to the hotel dining room. Hattie Bob saw her coming. "Now, just sit any-where you want or sit at the bar where I can serve you."

Louisa smiled at her and sat at the far end of the bar. She had the room to herself.

As she scanned the menu, Hattie Bob offered, "Listen, Sean can fix you a wonderful salad and grill a nice steak and a baked potato. All of that will surely fill that belly of yours."

Louisa smiled and nodded in the affirmative. "Medium will be fine," she said to Sean who was looking at her from the kitchen. He smiled as he began to fix her salad.

Now Hattie Bob was behind the bar looking at Louisa. "What would you like to go with the delicious meal Sean is preparing for you? Bet you're a red wine woman."

Louisa smiled at Hattie Bob. "Well, yes, I am. I have come to appreciate some wonderful red wines over the past several years. So, what have you lined up behind the bar?"

Hattie Bob laughed. "You ain't gonna find any ex-pensive French wines at this ole Hampton Inn. What I just got in is a nice red from Lodi, California. Believe it's a zinfandel. Let me see. Well, look at this, it's called Earthquake."

"Must be my lucky day because I have had Earthquake before, and I really like it."

Hattie Bob twisted out the cork and set a glass in front of Louisa. She carefully poured the wine into her glass. When she finished, Louisa held up her hand. "Just leave the bottle please."

Hattie Bob smiled as she set the bottle down in front of Louisa. She tuned and got the salad that Sean had set out. She looked at Louisa, but before she could say a word, Louisa said, "Oil and vinegar would be great."

It didn't take Louisa long to rip through the salad as well as the steak and baked potato. She gave Sean a thumbs up when she set her utensils down. He smiled and blushed a bit as she did.

She also made no waste of the wine as she drained the bottle. By that time, Hattie Bob had come and sat down behind the bar. "I could open another bottle, but I bet you might like something a little stronger. Let's see—are you a whiskey or a scotch drinker?"

Louisa didn't hesitate. "Scotch would be great!"

Hattie Bob tuned and produced an unopened bottle of Dewar's.

"On the rocks, please," Louisa offered before Hattie Bob could ask.

After Hattie Bob finished the pour, she sat and poured herself some of the same. "The kitchen is closed, and the night clerk just checked in. Time for my cocktail." She looked at Louisa. "So, Louisa Hawke, may I ask where you are going and what man are you leaving behind? While you were taking your shower, I googled your name, and—oh, my!—what a surprise. No, I'm not nosey or anything, but you just looked like an interesting person.

"Seems I have former FBI royalty here sitting in front to me. Now that is impressive. I just knew you were someone special when I first looked at you. But you're certainly not the run-of-the-mill single traveler who stops in to my Hampton Inn.

"From what I read, you and some man named Quinn McSpain were involved in some crazy stuff back in some place called Fancy Gap, Virginia. And all of that wasn't too long ago. I do hope you'll pardon me for being nosey, but I just had a feeling about you.

"So, here you are heading west without your McSpain fella, and you been crying a whole bunch. Now ole Hattie Bob ain't been to college, but I can just shut up and listen."

Louisa quickly welled up in tears, and she set her drink down. "Hattie Bob, I am such a . . . *fucking fool.*"

CHAPTER 4

Customs and Border Patrol Officer Leo Blais had just started his shift at the Jackman-Armstrong Maine Border Crossing. The line of cars, trucks, and buses coming toward the entry point into the United States from Canada seemed to be normal.

He looked at the white Mercedes van as it pulled up to his inspection station. Even though the afternoon light was fading, he quickly counted seven women in the van as well as a sole man who was driving. The van had Canadian license plates.

He looked at the driver. "Passports and vehicle registration please."

Traktor Berezin smiled and handed the seven passports from his passengers as well as his own to Officer Blais along with the van's registration forms.

Blais looked at the driver's passport first. He noticed they were all carrying British passports. He entered the driver's information into his computer system. The screen came alive and showed that Traktor Berezin had entered Canada from Great Britain some two weeks earlier. The same information came up for all of the seven women when he entered the information.

He looked at each of the women and saw that from their passport information, they were between the ages of nineteen and twenty-one. Yet as he looked at them more closely, he thought they looked a lot younger.

As he was doing that, his supervisor, Peter Beaulieu, came into his booth. Blais handed him the passports and made note of their ages.

Beaulieu looked closely at all the women. He then looked at Berezin. "Sir, can you tell me what your business is in the United States?"

"Officer, we are headed to Boston to attend the automobile convention that will be held there next week. We were in Quebec for a similar convention last week. The crew with me all work for me as models. We all live in London. I will be returning the van in Boston after the convention, and we will fly back to London."

Beaulieu turned to Blais's computer and through a Google search discovered that there was, indeed, an auto convention scheduled for the following week.

Blais looked at him and slid the window opening closed for a moment. "Pete, I just got a feeling about this group. The women in the van all look too young to be models."

Beaulieu turned and looked at all the women again. "Jesus, Leo, they are all gorgeous." He slid the window open again and looked at one of the passports. "Ms. Sokolov, how old are you?"

Elena swallowed hard. "I'm twenty-one years old, Officer," she replied in perfect English.

Beaulieu handed the passports back to Berezin and smiled. "Thank you, and have a safe trip while in the United States."

Berezin smiled as he took the passports. "Thank you very much. We will certainly enjoy your great country." He shifted the van back into drive and slowly entered the United States.

Blais and Beaulieu watched as the van pulled away. Blais spoke first. "Listen, there is something wrong with that group. He looked like a sex trafficking son of a bitch!"

Beaulieu nodded in agreement. "You might be right, Leo. Go ahead and highlight their information and pass it along to the ICE Predator Operation group in Portland. Let them run with this."

Blais winked at Beaulieu. "God, the girls were *freakin' georgous!*"

CHAPTER 5

QUINN MCSPAIN TURNED OFF THE LIVING ROOM TELEVI-
sion as the ten-thirty news ended. He knew what he
needed to do next. In a moment, he found his favorite
single-malt scotch. Two ice cubes clinked together as
they fell to the bottom of his glass.

He allowed himself a generous pour before he returned the cap to the bottle. This would be perfect for
the early cold front of Canadian air that moved in over
Fancy Gap. This was a night to be under the stars.

The door to the deck closed slowly behind him as he
rounded the corner to sit in his favorite spot. Two chairs
were placed side-by-side and faced the northern sky. He
sat in the chair on the left. The chair on the right was
empty.

Quinn took a long sip of scotch as he felt a chill from
the cold night air. It was the kind of night when you

could hear the stars breathing. The only silence was from the empty chair beside him.

Louisa was gone. Her absence left a hole in his very existence. He so wanted to feel her presence and meld into their oneness. He wondered if she would ever be in his arms again.

He second-guessed his decision to have her leave after her admission of her indiscretion. Yet he knew that only she could sort out what was troubling her torn heart.

Her attraction to the younger man she had met in Belize was something Quinn never saw coming. While they had been separated for several months, she never let on that a new man was in her life.

The notion that she might never return brought on a fear of emptiness that tore at the fabric of his very being. Yet his common sense dictated that he best prepare for that possibility.

A tear dropped off his cheek and silently splashed into his scotch. *He was . . . alone.*

———————

YURI DOBROW LOOKED AT HIS WATCH. HE KNEW THAT Traktor Berezin and his women should be close to the border of Canada and Maine. He was worried that he hadn't heard from them yet. While he didn't expect a problem at the border, he never discounted the possibility of the shit hitting the fan.

He stood and walked around the living room in the main building of the impressive compound. He built this place that was remote yet accessible to the clients that would come from all over and especially Washington to engage in their sexual fantasies. These clients would come from the business world as well as from the halls of Congress and the White House. He could guarantee their privacy and anonymity. Only he would know their identities.

Yes, this place called Pipers Gap was the perfect place to be hidden from the world. The construction was completed by contractors from North Carolina who were true to their craft. They were led to believe that this grand creation was for a Virginia millionaire who lived in Richmond.

The Carroll County authorities were pleased to see that the Mormons were building a retreat for members of the faith to visit from all over the United States. All permits were easily provided by the county.

The mile-long access road was well protected. A fortified gate controlled initial access. Within a quarter mile, a gate house was in place to verify the identity of all who passed through the gate. The entire fifty-acre complex was fenced and covered by state-of-the-art closed-circuit television system. Dogs roamed the fence line at night.

The 25,000-square-foot main building complex was built from plans designed to give the interior the look and feel of the Playboy Mansion in California. A grand ballroom was in the southern wing. The northern wing was comprised of seven magnificent bedrooms. While all different in style, each was equipped with opulent Jacuzzis and mirrored ceilings. The eastern wing was set as a bar and bistro. The western wing was equipped with pool tables and grand leather couches in front of a massive stone fireplace.

A separate ten-thousand-square-foot building was set a quarter mile away for the office functions, kitchen areas, and staff bedrooms. All vehicles were parked in a barn-like structure that could hold at least fifteen cars and trucks.

A heliport was set near the main complex. Not far from that in the front of the main building was a massive fifty-foot cross that highlighted the front of the complex. Its intent was to suggest the religious intent of the entire property.

Dobrow's phone vibrated as a new call came in. He saw Traktor's name displayed. "Well, my friend, I expect all things went well today?" he asked.

The voice on the other end of the line responded, "Without a hitch. We will be with you in ten hours. You will be happy to know that the precious cargo is *safe and sound!*"

HATTIE BOB LOOKED AT LOUISA. "NOW, MY INITIAL IM-pression of you, Louisa Hawke, is that you have rarely been a fool. No, I believe you have lived a very calculated life. I don't see a whole lot of nonsense in you or in any of your shit.

"So, do tell me what in tarnation happened to you that took you from your special place in wherever you live in Virginia to this here barstool your butt is sitting on?"

Louisa picked up a bar napkin and wiped the tears from her cheeks. "You're right, Hattie Bob. I have been cold and calculating for most of my adult life. I worked my ass off at the FBI and rose to the top because of it. I never let personal relationships get in the way of what I needed to accomplish. I was known as the coldest ice cube in the tray. Trust me, many took a run at me, but no one was allowed through the thicket I kept in their way.

"All of that was fine and dandy until a couple of years ago when out of the clear blue I met the man I was meant to fall in love with and be with. I never once thought I would meet such a man."

Hattie Bob leaned in a little closer. "How did this fella treat you?"

"Quinn McSpain has been the kindest and most lov-ing person on earth. He treats me like I'm the only wom-an on earth. We share intellectual delights and physical challenges that I never thought I would with any man."

Hattie Bob squinted a bit. "What about in the . . . you know what I mean."

Louisa smiled. "Hattie Bob, he satisfies my every sexual desire and fantasy. We meld into one when we come together, and I don't want it to ever end. He delivers. I never thought I would find a man who has taken me to places I never dreamed of!"

Hattie Bob took a deep breath. "Jeez, Louisa, I'm getting all hot and bothered just listening to you! Holy mackerel, how come I never met a man like that? Now listen, sister, how did you screw the pooch on this one?"

"Shit, I only wish I could take it all back. I was away from Quinn for eight or so weeks. I missed him dearly, and then I had this strapping young man some twenty years my junior who was paying attention to me. Or at least I thought he was.

"On one particularly warm and sultry night by a lake in northern Belize, I made the mistake of drinking some local moonshine with him by my side. Before I knew it, I was taking all my clothes off and we are skinny-dipping in the lake. It didn't take long before we were all wrapped up in each other, and he screwed my brains out. So, all of this lust exploded out of me, and the moonshine made me looney.

"I woke up the next day and looked at him all naked in the water again, and I didn't know what to think. I suggested to him that it was very special, and he stated that it was only sex and nothing more.

"So, then I suddenly had to leave Belize, and I was confused. I got back to Fancy Gap and told Quinn that I was confused. He suggested in no uncertain terms that I leave and not come back till I sort things out. And here I am with you."

Hattie Bob opened another bottle of Dewar's and filled both of their glasses. "Louisa, honey, I believe I know what the problem is here. Yours truly here has been married three times. Divorced twice and the third kicked the bucket. During and in between, I engaged in an activity that certainly has been absent from your sexually cloistered life. What I'm referring to is sport sex. That bit of freelance activity has been most enjoyable on many occasions. Now the key to sport fucking is that both parties must agree that you are both having sex . . . just for fun. No strings attached, ya see.

"That works out just fine if all are discreet and ya don't lose your mind and think it's love. No, it is lust and only lust. As I see it, that's what that fella in Belize was thinking about. He got aroused around little ole you and decided to lighten his load a bit. Slam, bam, thank you, ma'am. Once the sex was over, that was it. Over and done. Finished and thank you.

"But there you were, all liquored up and all this sex with this young stud made you think you were in love. That might be a natural reaction for a woman, no matter her age, especially one like you who didn't have any experience with sport sex."

Louisa took a long sip of her scotch and thought for a moment. She rolled her eyes and began to laugh. "Hattie Bob, why in the devil didn't I take that course so much sooner in life! Guess that only makes sense, doesn't it? I run into a young stud and I think I've caught the love bug."

Louisa stood and laughed as she went around the bar and hugged Hattie Bob. "Thank you for these last three hours. A lot of things make much more sense now. I was a fool, and it has cost me dearly."

Hattie Bob smiled. "Louisa, go on up to your room and sleep on all of this. While I have never met your Quinn, I bet he just might be willing to let you *back into his heart!*"

CHAPTER 6

YURI DOBROW'S CELL PHONE VIBRATED FOR A SECOND. The text message from the front security gate informed him that the van had arrived. He passed on the text to Anatoly Kristoff and Sasha Petrov and asked them to be in the main room in ten minutes. He looked at his watch and was impressed that they had arrived by nine at night.

Dobrow had orchestrated similar operations in Berlin and London. The information that was secured from those politicians and business leaders who succumbed to their sexual fantasies was priceless. That information was useful at gaining leverage in future business or political transactions.

Traktor Berezin drove slowly around the winding road to the main compound and looked in the rearview mirror. All the young women seemed to be awake or just waking up. Lights lit up the roadway as he approached.

He pulled to the side of the roadway just before he reached the end. The view of the main compound from that spot was magnificent. He put the van in park and turned to look at the girls. "All of you look at this wonderful building, as this is your new home. You are truly blessed to have been chosen for this assignment. Many would have given so much to have this opportunity."

None of the girls responded as they gazed at all of the buildings that were all lit up with exterior spotlights.

Elena Sokolov looked at Natalia Popov. "This is truly a beautiful place!"

Popov didn't respond.

Berezin started the van and drove to the main entrance. He stepped out of the van and opened the large side door. All the seven girls slid out one after another. They continued to look around before the two massive oak doors to the main compound opened.

Yuri Dobrow stepped outside on the top step and smiled. He immediately realized that all the seven girls were much more beautiful than in their pictures. He opened his arms in a welcoming gesture. "My dearest children, welcome to your new home—our little spot of paradise.

"You are the chosen few who have been selected to live a new and wonderful life. Now come inside to meet your new family!" He watched all the girls slowly walk by and immediately knew which would be the first to feel his . . . *passion.*

LEROY ALMOST JUMPED BACK OUT OF HIS CHAIR. HE caught the side of his desk before he fell. He could not stop staring at the clear cylinder sitting on his desk. He slowly reached for his magnifying glass and held it closer to the cylinder. "Dang, Levi, you're right. There is a shriveled-up penis in that darn tube! What in the Lord's name is this all about?"

Levi shook his head from side to side. "Holy moly, Leroy. I'm getting a not-so-pretty flashback! This has gotta be related to when we found that poor kid strapped to the gate at the Devil's Den opening. Remember, his penis was cut off, and we never found it!"

Leroy listened as his mind took him back to the very first encounter he'd had had with the Preston family. They were traveling south to Florida from Michigan to attend a funeral. It was late afternoon when they reached the Hillsville/Fancy Gap area on Interstate 77.

The father disregarded the posted fog advisory and quickly was part of the highway mayhem that killed and injured more than a few. Luckily, he and his wife as well as their two children were not injured.

They found lodging that night in the old motel in Fancy Gap. Unbeknownst to them, a madman was lurking in the bushes with every intent of kidnapping a child. As fate would have it, the lunatic managed to capture both children. And as the world would soon find out, the madman was the local Catholic priest.

While the little boy, Pete, was killed by the priest, the sister, Katie, stayed in captivity until she was freed when Quinn McSpain and Louisa Hawke worked with the sheriff to find the missing girl. In the end, the sheriff was the one to kill the madman.

The sheriff slowly sat back in his chair. "That boy was Pete Preston. Our mad killer priest killed that boy and set him there for all to see. I have always wondered what happened to that missing part of his anatomy. I remember we searched for days to find his missing penis. When we went through what was left of the priest's belongings, there was nothing to be found then."

Levi quickly jumped in, "And I always thought that his no-account adopted son, Tommie Cruz, might have had it. But then again, I thought it might have been destroyed when he blew up his place in Galax."

The sheriff rubbed his forehead with both hands. "So, Levi, what does this mean? It's been awhile since you killed Tommie Cruz. Now all of a sudden this shows up with a note from a dead man. So, it doesn't take a genius to deduct that ole dead Tommie Cruz has an accomplice who has been lying in the weeds for some time now."

Levi reached for his cell phone. "Leroy, I'm going to call our medical examiner to see if he can connect some dots here. Dr. Kahn can help us with this 'cause we need to know who was the rightly owner of this shriveled *whatever*!"

———◆———

QUINN STARED INTO HIS COMPUTER AND FLIPPED through all of the travel options on the Travelzoo website. He knew a change of scenery was in order. Before he could hit the next key, his growling stomach got the best of him. He shut his computer down and headed out of the door.

It took all of five minutes for him to reach the Fancy Gap Deli located at the entrance to the Blue Ridge Parkway in Fancy Gap. He enjoyed eating there, as he liked the staff as well as the delicious deli treats and homemade pies.

As usual, the parking lot at the deli was full. Locals as well as tourists traveling down the Blue Ridge Parkway knew the deli was a good place to stop for quick and wholesome meals.

Quinn never saw the Porsche 911T parked on the other side of a parked motor home. He looked around the parking lot and admired the late fall colors adorning the tree line. This was by far his favorite time of year.

He walked through the entrance and immediately caught the eye of Sharon, who managed the deli. She only smiled a half-smile when she saw him. Her eyes shifted to the corner table in the far side of the deli.

His eyes followed her until they rested on a man and woman sitting at the table. He immediately recognized the woman but did not know the man. By chance, Libby Thomas turned her head at that very moment and saw Quinn standing there.

She jumped up and waved him over to her table. Quinn could see Sharon roll her eyes as she looked away. For a moment, Quinn considered turning around and leaving, but his stomach got the better of him.

Libby Thomas was the wealthiest woman in Carroll County and probably in all of southwest Virginia as well. Some speculated that she was at least in the top five of the richest women in all of Virginia. She owned most of the independent banks in the area as well as multiple successful industrial parks from Richmond, Virginia, all the way to Miami, Florida.

She also was a woman of considerable beauty who looked half her age. Her iron will and ability to have her own way were legendary in the various business communities she chose to be in. If she wanted something, she bought it or destroyed it if she could not add it to her considerable stable.

Much to her dismay, the only man she really coveted and desired yet could not have was standing in the deli doorway. She understood the love Quinn McSpain had for Louisa Hawke, and while she had tried, she could never separate the two. That was, up until now.

Libby waved frantically at Quinn, who offered a tepid wave in response as he slowly headed toward her table. He looked around and saw that all the tables in the deli were occupied. In a moment, he was standing in front of Libby.

She jumped up and gave him a warm hug. "Listen, you big hunk, you have to sit right down and have lunch with me."

Quinn turned his eyes to the man sitting at her table in an expensive business suit taking a bite of a sandwich.

"Oh, Quinn, this is Sam Longo from Atlanta, who is trying to convince me to buy his business. Sam was about to leave, as we are meeting tomorrow to review his numbers."

It became evident to Sam that his lunch was over. He stood and extended his hand to Libby, which she ignored. He looked at Quinn. "Have a nice afternoon," he muttered as he wiped his chin and walked out.

Libby quickly moved the half-eaten sandwich aside and motioned for Sharon to come to her table.

Quinn sat in the now vacant chair and looked at Libby and shook his head. "Libby, that was downright rude. That poor man hadn't finished his sandwich. He might not forgive you for that."

Libby lost her smile. "That man once had a lot of money. But because of lust and bad gambling habits, he is now on the brink of sliding into an unforgiving financial shithole. He is here because he has what I want. He has two spectacular young thoroughbreds that would be a nice addition to my farm. I will give him twenty cents on the dollar to buy his businesses. And he will throw in the two horses.

"That will save his face and his family for now. But it won't be long before Sam blows the money on his expensive girlfriend and her cocaine habits. But that, my dear friend Quinn, is not my problem. So, you see, I'm not a bad person, but I make the most of opportunities that come my way. To Sam, I am an angel!"

Libby did not see Sharon standing behind her, taking in every word. Quinn just shook his head while Sharon spoke, "Quinn, you just have that hungry man look on your face. What can I get for you, sweetie?"

"Your delicious chicken salad sandwich and some onion rings would be great."

Sharon smiled, "Now, Quinn, you make sure you eat that sandwich quickly when it gets here 'cause no telling when Ms. Libby will shoo you away."

Libby tuned beet red for a moment as Sharon walked back to the kitchen. "That woman just gets under my skin. I wish I could buy this place, so I could fire her! Well, enough about her. How are you getting along, dear Quinn? I understand that your Louisa flew the coop as they say. Is that true, or am I indulging myself in wishful thinking?"

Quinn waited a moment before he answered. "Libby don't believe all you hear. Louisa has taken—well, how can I put this—she is on a sabbatical. Sometimes one needs to sort things out that can only be done in one's own solitude."

Libby leaned in a little closer to Quinn. Her physical assets were on full display. "How are you getting along without her? I know she has been gone for a little bit. Any idea if she will ever return? I don't want you to think I'm nosey or anything like that, but I'm concerned about you. I would love to spend some quality time with you, and I would surely do my best to make you very happy."

She was inching even closer to Quinn when Sharon came to the table with his meal. "Move aside, blondie, 'cause this man needs to eat." Libby seethed as Sharon put his plate in front of him. As she did, she looked at him. "Quinn, tomorrow is my day off, and I'm going into Winston-Salem. I would love some company, and I could buy you dinner at one of those fancy restaurants down there."

Quinn thought Libby's eyes would burst out of their sockets when he took Sharon's hand. "Let me think about that 'cause I have a few things I need to pick up at the Sam's Club down there."

Sharon slowly pivoted and cocked her head back as she looked at Libby. "I'll call you tonight to set the time."

Quinn took another bite of his sandwich before Libby spoke. "McSpain, there will come a point in time when you realize I'm the right woman for you. You know I get what I want, and you are at the top of my list. I'm usually not a patient person, but for you, I will bite my tongue and wait for that very moment when you realize I'm the one for you!"

With those final words, she stood and planted a big kiss on Quinn's cheek. By then, all eyes of the patrons in the deli were upon her as she rose and sashayed slowly out of the restaurant.

Quinn smiled as he finished off his sandwich. At that very moment his iPhone rang. It was *the sheriff.*

CHAPTER 7

Hattie Bob was busy keeping up with the hotel guests who were checking out. As soon as she finished with the couple who were now going out the front door, she looked up from her computer screen.

Louisa smiled as their eyes met.

"By golly, look who's on the move. I haven't seen you in two whole days, and now it looks like you're ready to hit the road. I can only wonder in which direction your tormented soul is headed, girl?"

"After that talking to you gave me the other night and the soul searching I've been through in the last for-ty-eight hours, I know what direction I need to go in. I was a fool, and I darn well know it.

"So, me and that Volvo of mine are heading back to that very special place I miss and the man I love. I only hope it's not too late and he can find some way to forgive me," Louisa offered as she wiped a tear from her cheek.

Hattie Bob walked around the desk and took Louisa in her arms. "My dearest, this is the right thing to do. I think your Quinn fella is no fool. He more than likely will give you a pass for your little dalliance. Now turn right around and get on the road 'cause a good man is waiting for you in that fancy place in Virginia!"

Louisa walked to the front door. She turned and waved to Hattie Bob as the door closed behind her. Hattie Bob smiled and wiped a tear from her cheek as she watched Louisa drive away.

A man who was patiently waiting to check out asked, "Is that a special goodbye service of this place?"

Hattie Bob looked at him. "*You should be so lucky!*"

ALL THE SEVEN YOUNG WOMEN FOLLOWED SASHA PETROV into a small conference room. They saw a round table in the middle of the room and seven chairs equally spaced apart. There were name cards with each of their names place in front of the chairs.

Petrov spoke, "Ladies, find your places at the table and be seated."

As each sat, they looked at a tray sitting in front of their name cards. Each tray was overflowing with expensive diamond rings and necklaces as well as other precious stones. None of the girls touched the jewelry.

Petrov walked through an opening in the table and stood in the middle of the circle. "My dearest daughters, please do touch and try on what you see in front of you, as this is all yours."

Elena Sokolov looked at Natalia Popov, who was sitting next to her, as she attached a diamond necklace around her neck. Natalia picked up a hand mirror from the table and held it in front of Elena.

Both giggled as Elena's mouth opened wide in awe. She had never seen anything like this. All of the young women were quickly consumed with trying on and admiring every piece that was before them.

Petrov waited for a good ten minutes before she spoke. "Ladies, how very special you all look. Now set your jewelry down and listen to me. To begin, what you have in front of you is all real. There is over a million dollars in jewels on this table.

"This is, as they say in English, the tip of the iceberg. When you leave and go to your rooms, you will find some of the most beautiful clothes a woman could ever dream of owning. Don't be surprised to find that everything will fit you. Dresses, underwear, blouses, shoes— yes, all will fit.

"Your new mother has thought of everything. I'm sure that while you drove here Traktor explained that there are very strict rules each of you must follow. It is vital that you follow the rules.

"This is not a prison. I will take some of you out to shop with me based on your performance. But you will have all you need right here in your new home.

"I know you are wondering how long you will be here. That answer is simple. If you follow the rules and perform at an exemplary level, you will return to Mother Russia in two years. If you break the rules and cause problems, you will leave earlier . . . *in a box!*"

———

DR. KAHN WAS THE CARROLL COUNTY MEDICAL EXAMINER. He had held that position for over twenty-five years. He had already announced that he planned to retire at the end of the year. He also planned to end his successful medical practice. His only daily prayer was that he didn't have to get involved in any sort of catastrophe before the end of the year.

He cringed a bit when he saw Levi Blackburn's name on his cell phone screen. He didn't normally receive social calls from Levi. He hit the answer button. "Levi, I hope this call is to schedule some time for us to play a round of golf!"

"No, Doc, not this time. Need you to come to the sheriff's office 'bout as quick as you can. Leroy got a package in the mail, and it's something you need to see."

"Dang, Levi, do I get a hint?" the good doctor asked.

"No, you sure nuff don't. 'Cause you wouldn't believe me if I told you. What I can tell you is that it looks like someone done lost his *putter!*"

LIBBY SAT IN HER PORSCHE AND FUMED, BUT NOT FOR long. Her lust for McSpain took over as she sped out of the deli parking lot and turned onto the Blue Ridge Parkway. Within minutes, she was speeding around State Road 608. It didn't take long for her to get to her intended destination.

She knew of the abandoned back road that ended near Quinn's house. Once at the end, she cut off the Porsche and got out. She was certain Quinn would not see her car as he drove back to his house.

She started to walk slowly toward his house but picked up the pace, as she wanted to be there before he arrived. She slowed as she rounded the bottom of the hill leading to his hot tub.

Once in front of it, she opened the power box and threw the switch. In a moment, the two five-horsepower Emerson Electric motors came to life, and the forty jets spit out streams of water.

In one fluid motion, she flipped the hot tub cover off and started to unbutton her blouse. Her slacks and underwear followed. She smiled as she heard a vehicle coming up the dirt road.

Her naked body submerged into the tub as the warm water started to circulate and the jets massaged her back. She saw Quinn's truck pull into the driveway.

Quinn parked his truck and walked up the porch and into the house. He looked at his phone to see if there were any messages. There weren't any. He thought about going out back to split wood for the fireplace.

That thought was quickly lost, as he knew he needed a soak in the hot tub. He glanced at the wine rack in the kitchen and knew it was time to liberate his favorite zinfandel from its bottle.

As soon as he filled his glass, he headed to his bedroom to undress. He looked at his robe but decided that all he needed was his wine glass. Before he reached the lower level, he was almost certain he heard his hot tub running.

He opened the lower porch door and slowly walked over to the tub. He looked beyond the top that was off to the side but did not see anyone in the tub. He leaned over to get a better look only to be startled when Libby's head slowly emerged from the water.

The surprise of the moment was quickly interrupted as Libby slowly slid up and stood not some two feet away from him. She reached out and took the wine glass from his hand.

"Oh, my dearest Quinn, how thoughtful of you to bring a thirsty lady a glass of nice wine." She leaned forward and kissed him on the cheek.

Quinn was at a loss for words as he admired her naked torso. She slowly slithered back into the tub.

"Now be a good boy and go back and get yourself a glass of wine so we can drink together." Libby licked her lips before dipping her finger into the glass and spread the wine over her lips. She sat up a bit as her ample and firm breasts broke the water line and seemed to be staring at Quinn.

Quinn gulped as he pivoted and headed to the door. He bounded up the stairs and headed to his bedroom, where he slipped on his robe. He only paused for a moment as he headed back to the kitchen and poured another glass of wine.

He headed back downstairs, now somewhat more composed as he tied his robe at the waist and headed out toward the hot tub. Within a few steps, he saw that Libby was now sitting on the edge of the tub with her long legs crossed.

Quinn sat on the other edge from where she was sitting. Libby was the first to speak. "Now, now, dear boy, why the robe? I loved seeing you in all your nakedness. You look too good to be covered up."

Quinn swallowed hard before he spoke. "Libby, let me be brutally frank with you. If I weren't so in love with

Louisa, I would slide into that tub and screw your brains out. You're beautiful and as seductive as a woman can be. Yet I know who I love."

Libby took a slow sip of wine. As she did, she unfolded her legs and slowly spread them apart, leaving nothing to the imagination. "You are smitten with her, and I know that. But where is she? I know what she did in Belize. She wasn't faithful to you.

"Yet you sit here with every opportunity to share your sexy self with a woman who truly appreciates you and can give you the world. Live in the moment, Quinn, and let me give you what you deserve. She's gone, and I'm but a moment away from living in your fantasy and making you forget about Louisa."

Quinn watched her take another sip and start to message her ample breast with her other hand. He felt a stirring in his groin began to take shape. He swallowed hard again before he spoke. "Libby, you have so much to give, but not to me. Perhaps at another place in time, this might have worked."

As he spoke, Libby slid off the edge she was sitting on and slowly moved in his direction. She stopped within inches of his face and started to caress his ear with her tongue.

Her other hand found its way under his robe and slowly began to slide upward. Quinn suppressed a moan as he inched back a foot away from her. His right hand took the wine glass from her.

"Libby, you will never know how close you just came to whatever you desire. But close is all you get. Do feel free to sit in the tub as long as you want, but I'm going back into the house."

With that, he pivoted on one foot and headed back to the porch door. Libby heard the screen door close as he slid back into the tub. "Damn you, Quinn McSpain! I will have my way with you yet!"

She lifted one leg out of the tub and paused. She smiled as her stream of urine splashed into the tub. *"Piss on you, McSpain!"*

CHAPTER 8

SHE SAT NAKED ON HER BED AND LOOKED AROUND HER bedroom. Her sadness was set deep in the furthest corner of her heart. The man she loved had been brutally taken from her, and she was helpless to do anything about it.

No one in southwest Virginia was sad when Tommie Cruz was killed by Levi Blackburn, the Carroll County detective. To all who cared, he was a ruthless killer who was out to avenge the death of his adopted father, who was a Catholic priest.

She was convinced that no one on the face of the earth knew she'd had an affair with Tommie Cruz. While he pursued other women in Galax and throughout the county, she knew that no one could ever know of their relationship.

His death left a hole in her life. Yet she was still faithful to his desires even after death, as he knew that his life could be cut short at any time during his quest to kill Quinn McSpain and Louisa Hawke. While she never felt any hatred toward those two, she understood what Tommie felt.

She thought of all of that when she followed the instructions that Tommie had left with the small package he had put in her safe. She waited the exact amount of days that Tommie had suggested before she went to the UPS store in Mount Airy, North Carolina.

She was cautious to disguise her identity when she arrived at the store. She wore a wig and parked a good distance away. She paid with cash and wore gloves the entire time.

She didn't know what was in the package and didn't care. Tommie would have told her if he would have wanted her to know. She knew she would soon find out exactly what was in the package that was addressed to the Carroll County sheriff.

In the past, she had passed a lot of private and confidential information from the sheriff's department to Tommie. That information was useful in his quest to kill McSpain and Hawke.

She stood and looked at her nakedness in the mirror on the back of her bedroom door. The thought of how

Tommie would look at her and have his way with her stirred passionate thoughts.

The alarm on her iPhone reminded her that she had thirty minutes to get ready for work. She dressed quickly and headed out the door and knew she would arrive in no time for her job at the . . . *sheriff's department.*

———— ◆ ————

QUINN HIT THE ANSWER BUTTON ON HIS CELL PHONE. "So, what makes me so special that the high sheriff of Carroll County would be calling me?"

Leroy laughed before he spoke. "Well, McSpain, I was just thinking of all the folks I might know who might have lost something recently." Before he finished, he realized that was the wrong thing to say.

"Leroy, you got your man. I just lost the opportunity to shack up with Libby Thomas. That woman is just determined to get into my pants."

"McSpain, I'm happy you said that because I thought you might have thought I was referring to Louisa. Libby Thomas is a whole other matter. Good to hear that you kept her fangs at bay.

"But listen—there is a something you need to see. Can you come by the office like right now?"

There was a slight pause on the other end. "Be there in ten minutes, Sheriff."

Quinn scratched his chin as he backed his truck up and wondered exactly what new mystery the sheriff might drag him into. *He would soon find out.*

RUFUS AND GEARLEEN SURRATT SAT ON THE SIDE OF the mountain overlooking the large complex with the supersized cross. They had been sitting there for hours without a word spoken to each other.

Both Rufus and Gearleen were born in Carroll County. Rufus was born in the Pipers Gap district, whereas Gearleen grew up in the Fancy Gap district. While in the senior year in high school, they'd met on a Friday night at the Fancy Gap Auction House.

While there was nothing particularly attractive about either, a bond based on simplicity soon developed, and they were married after they graduated from high school. They both began working together at the Hanes Underwear plant in Galax, Virginia.

By all accounts, both were pleased with their jobs at the plant and would have continued to work there—until the plant closed. Rufus decided to start his own grass cutting and landscaping business. Gearleen got a job at the Burger King in downtown Hillsville.

Neither Rufus nor Gearleen were particularly social. They never had children and didn't have any pets.

Their main recreation was spending long hours hiking and exploring the countryside in Carroll County as well as the surrounding counties.

At this point in time, their interest was drawn to the five hundred or so acres of land that had once belonged to the Shelor clan. Rufus didn't know that the land had been sold until two years past when a North Carolina construction company began clearing the land.

The scuttlebutt around Pipers Gap was that some large religious organization had bought the land. But, as Rufus soon found out, no one knew for sure. Hardly a weekend went by that Rufus and Gearleen didn't sit on their perch deep in the woods and try to see as much as they could.

The problem they encountered was that not much of the forest canopy was cut down. Thus, it was difficult to see very much. They passed the binoculars back and forth to see as much as they could.

When most of the construction was completed, they drove from their house up to the new front gate that was now in place. Once they got there, Rufus parked near the gate and got out of his truck.

Before he got close to the gate, a man walked through the metal turnstile and approached Rufus. The man asked Rufus if he could help him in any way. Rufus asked if there was a chance anyone could find work at this new compound.

The man was polite and told Rufus that all the jobs had been filled and he didn't expect to be any openings in the foreseeable future. He took out a pad of paper and asked Rufus for his cell number so he could call if a vacancy occurred.

Rufus smiled and explained to the man that he did not have a cell phone as of yet, but he did pass along the landline number at his house. The man wrote it down and thanked Rufus for his interest.

When the man stopped talking, Rufus knew it was time to leave. He thought about shaking the man's hand but decided the man didn't appear to be the hand-shaking type.

Rufus walked back to the truck, opened the door, and slid into the driver's seat. He stared straight ahead until Gearleen said, "What did the fella tell you? They got jobs for us or not?"

Rufus continued to look straight ahead. "There were three other fellas in that there gate house. And they had them some mighty powerful rifles and pistols. The fella I spoke with had a nine-millimeter pistol under his jacket. But no matter, Gearleen—that man could have killed me with his hands."

Gearleen listened. "Okay by that, but darn, Rufus, what did he say about any jobs?"

Rufus turned and looked at her. "Nope, not a darn thing at the present, he told me. But he took down our telephone number and promised to call if something opens up."

That encounter was the reason Rufus and Gearleen were now sitting on the ridge. They had convinced themselves that there was more to see on the inside of the compound. They had been sitting for several hours when they knew it was time to get back to their house to watch their favorite television shows. As they began the hike back to their truck, they heard a vehicle approaching along the long access road.

Rufus took the binoculars and caught a glimpse of the large passenger van as it rounded a corner. He only caught a glimpse of what he thought was several women in the van.

Before he could hand the binoculars to Gearleen, the van disappeared along the curvy road.

Gearleen looked at him. "I think we should follow the fence line to see what in tarnation is happening in that place."

Rufus thought for a moment. "Gearleen, that means we might miss *The Price is Right* and a few other shows."

Geraleen took his hand as she headed toward the upper ridge that followed the fence line. Within ten minutes, they came down off the ridge and started to inch closer to the spot near the fence line where they could get a better view of the compound.

They slowly crept along to where they thought was the best vantage point. Rufus slowly brought the binoculars up to his eyes. In a moment, he felt something nudge his head.

As he turned to see what was happening, he looked right into Gearleen's eyes, which were wide open. A large man was holding her still with a long knife pressed to her throat.

He looked the other way before his lights *went out*.

———

YURI DOBROW LOOKED AT HIS COMPUTER SCREEN AND smiled. His brother, Andrei, who worked at the Russian Embassy in Washington, was putting the finishing touches on the next gathering in Pipers Gap.

The Bratva had done their homework and had discreetly found several high-ranking members of the White House staff as well as members of Congress who had some history of sexual deviations that now could be exploited.

Most of those interested had heard of ultra-secret gatherings in Europe and Asia where even the wildest sexual fantasies were acted upon in the most discreet ways in secret locations. Now, through casual conversations with trusted associates, the word among a select few seemed to indicate that this opportunity might be available in the United States.

Many who were in the small circle of those contacted backed away immediately. They understood the potential risks that could explode into scandal. All in male bastions of business or political power were frightened by the current #MeToo movement and the inherent lack of due process.

Yet the Bratva understood the sheer urge to live out secret sexual fantasies that even the most cautious might be attracted to. The ability to believe that the risks were particularly nonexistent would be the deciding factor in making the decision to attend.

Yuri smiled when he looked at the several names that had committed to the offering. None seemed to balk at the cost of $50,000. All had managed to find a way to pay in the bitcoin currency. He printed off a copy of the report his brother had sent.

He looked at his watch and realized he was late for a planning meeting with Sasha, Traktor, and Anatoly Kristoff, their security chief. They were all present when he entered his small conference room. He looked at each of them as he passed out copies of the report.

"As you will see, my brother Andrei did a superb job with the planning for the next gathering. Several high-ranking government officials as well as a few select business executives have paid for their trips into fantasy land.

"So, the seven individual nights have been set. The very first person will be picked up by our helicopter at a rendezvous point just outside of Washington. I will meet the helicopter when it arrives. As is our procedure, our special guest will be blindfolded for the last hour of flight.

"Sasha, you will have all the seven girls ready and in place for the arrival. I expect our guest to enjoy the most memorable twenty-four hours of pure fantasy. Let's plan to have a walk-through with the girls at least a day before the guest arrives. Anatoly, ensure that all covert cameras and microphones are in place and operative. Every moment of the experience must be secured."

Anatoly Kristoff shook his head. "Not to worry, Yuri. When Tommie Cruz set this system up, he left nothing to chance. Every moment will be captured."

Traktor frowned at the remark. "True, my brother, but your Mr. Cruz wasn't so lucky when he lost his life to the police."

Anatoly held up his hand. "That is true. He was shot by the police. But what he provided to us before that was invaluable. We know that his equipment is superb. All of our communication systems are very secure. No agency or government can penetrate our defenses. Even in death, he is helping us. He did pass along the name of the person who was his mole in the local sheriff's department. That, my friends, might be of use to us in the future."

As he finished that statement, his cell phone buzzed. He immediately answered the call. Within a moment, he hung up. "That was the exterior patrol. They caught a man and a woman along the fence line who were trying to observe our operations. They are being brought to our secure detention room."

Yuri turned beet red. "Go, Anatoly, and find out *what the fuck is going on!*"

———————

Quinn parked his truck in the Carroll County Sheriff Department parking lot. Before he could shut the engine off, a car pulled alongside of him. He smiled as he saw Dr. Kahn jump out of his car.

Before he could open his door, Dr. Kahn walked over and pulled his door open. "I guess I'm not at all surprised to see you here, McSpain. By the tone in Levi's voice when he called me, I suspected some shit had hit the fan. Do you have a clue as to why they called us?"

"No, Doc, I don't. The sheriff called and asked me to come to his office. I guess it did sound urgent. But I don't have the faintest idea. But here we both are, so my first tendency is to say that something bad happened."

"No doubt about that, Quinn. This will not be a social call. But listen, before we go up the office, can I ask if you have heard anything from Louisa? I understand if you don't want to discuss, but I do worry 'bout you two."

"Doc, thanks for asking. The simple answer is no. Nothing since she left. I don't know where she went. I suspect she might be driving to California to see her sister. But I have no way of knowing."

Doctor Kahn patted him on the shoulder as they walked into the sheriff's office. Levi got up from his desk as he saw them walk into Leroy's office. The sheriff finished a call and hung up his phone.

Levi jumped into the last empty chair when all were seated at the sheriff's office table. Leroy looked at Quinn and Dr. Khan. "So, this has been an outrageous day already. Take a look at the package on the middle of this table. It was delivered this morning."

With that, he reached over, picked up the package, and unwrapped it. He then handed the cylinder to Dr. Kahn. "Take a good look at that, Doc. Then give it to Quinn to look at."

Dr. Kahn slowly twirled the cylinder between his fingers. He then took out what looked like a small cigar case holder from his breast pocket. He opened it up and removed a small flashlight. He pushed the bottom button, and it lit up.

He twirled the cylinder with the light shining through. Quinn watched closely until the doc finished and handed the cylinder over to him. Quinn held it up to the light and slowly spun it around. Within a minute, he set it down.

Leroy looked at Dr. Kahn. "What do you think, Doc?"

"While I'm not 100 percent sure, my bet is that this is what remains of one young Pete Preston. And I do speculate that this is the missing penis. I will do all the necessary testing to confirm that bit of speculation, but I'm pretty sure that will back up my assumption."

Quinn looked at them and shook his head. "I agree with our good friend here; that must be the missing penis. But why the hell should it show up now?"

Levi jumped into the conversation, "Read the note, Quinn. . . . Just read the note!"

Quinn took the paper and looked at the writing. "'You motherfuckers might have killed me, but you will feel my wrath from the depths of hell. Tommie Cruz.'"

He handed the note to Doctor Kahn. He read it and shook his head.

The sheriff stood and shook his head. "So, what the heck is going on here, fellas? A note from a dead man along with a penis from a dead boy? This is insane! What the hell is going on here?"

All were quiet for a moment before Quinn spoke. "First of all, it doesn't make any sense. Unless, of course, we jump to the assumption that someone somewhere is a sympathetic friend to Tommie Cruz. And that person carried out his wish to have us see this. But why? Is there yet another person out there who hates us and wants to kill us?"

Levi twitched from side to side as he usually did when he was in deep thought. "Fellas, this ain't good. No damn good at all! My gut feeling is that someone close to us is responsible for all of this. Now I gotta think 'bout this for a good while before I can take it somewhere."

The doc looked at Levi. "Dang, Levi, that is a pretty interesting thought, but really? I just don't know."

The sheriff was about to say something when Quinn's phone beeped in a loud tone. Quinn looked at the screen and stood. "I need to leave. There's a car *in my driveway!*"

———

ELENA AND NATALIA WERE EXHAUSTED AFTER SPENDING two hours working out in the spacious gym. Every piece of modern workout equipment was set in the room. All the girls were encouraged to work out on a daily basis.

Natalia wasn't fond of the daily workout routine. She was pleased that Elena did her best to make sure she didn't miss a day. They both knew that Sasha would get a report if any of the girls missed working out two days in a row.

Elena finished her shower first and was drying her hair when Natalia stepped out of the shower. Elena admired her perfect figure and long, jet-black hair. Natalia laughed when she realized Elena was looking at her.

"Don't worry, my sweet friend. All the men we will soon bring pleasure to will love your creamy white skin and perfect breasts as well as your auburn hair. They might not even look at me at all!"

Elena started to laugh at her comment. "I will be lucky to find any man interested in me at all if you are in the same room. Sasha might even send me home if no one is interested."

"There is no chance of that. And besides, why would you want to leave all of this? We all had less-than-desirable lives back in Mother Russia. No one had what we have now, Elena. Look at our room and our clothes, and what do we have to do? Have sex with some old and stupid men while we don't even think about it."

"But, Natalia, what have we given up? We are prisoners here! We have no freedom at all. If we try to leave, they will kill our parents and brothers and sisters. I know we will not be here forever, but what will happen when they have no use for us? Will they kill us?"

Natalia stood and took Elena's hand. "Come with me. Let's go back to my room and listen to music and think happier thoughts."

Elena smiled as she stood and took Natalia's hand.

Yuri watched from his office and immediately knew it was time to act on the desire that swelled below his belt. Within two minutes, he was rounding the corner leading to the wing where the girls' rooms were located.

He was wearing gym shorts and a tight-fitting t-shirt. Elena and Natalia stopped in their tracks as they rounded the corner and stood directly in front of him. They smiled, as they clearly understood that Yuri was in charge and he could determine their fate on a whim. Sasha had also told them to do whatever he desired.

Yuri smiled as he looked at them both. "Are you both busy right now?" he asked.

Elena looked at him without changing her expression. "We were going to my room to listen to music."

Natalia squeezed her hand tightly. "But we certainly can do that later if you need us for something right now."

Yuri reached between them and took their hands in his. "I think I do need both of you right now. Let's take a walk together."

Within five minutes, they were at the entrance of the indoor grotto water garden. Water gently flowed over small waterfalls into small wading pools that were bathed in soft underwater lights.

The room smelled of lavender, and the room was filled with soft music. The girls had seen the grotto but had not yet been in the water.

Yuri led them to the sunken center of the grotto. He smiled as he slowly removed his t-shirt and let his shorts drop to the floor. "Now you must show me what you will do when you are with guests in this lovely place."

Elena looked and was somewhat impressed with his level of physical fitness. Natalia wasted no time in slowly taking her top off and smiling as she turned and pulled Elena in closer to her.

She smiled as she slipped Elena's top up and over her head. Her hands then slid down Elena's shoulders to settle on her firm breasts. Her forefingers squeezed Elena's nipples.

Elena began to breathe harder as Natalia began to kiss her breasts and tickled the nipples with her tongue. Elena quickly responded, pulled Natalia in closer, and passionately kissed her.

Natalia smiled as she looked at Yuri, who was now fully aroused and was stroking himself. She slowly pulled herself away from Elena and walked the few steps to stand in front of Yuri.

She slowly pulled her shorts down while licking her lips. As she stepped out of her shorts, she knelt in front of Yuri. She took his manliness and slowly licked and kissed his manhood.

Elena could hear Yuri moan as Natalia worked her magic. Yuri watched Elena strip off her shorts as she approached them both. She knelt behind Natalia and gently messaged her buttocks.

Natalia understood what might happen next as she tilted her butt up higher and felt Elena work her magic.

Elena felt Natalia's satisfaction as moisture flowed from her now-gyrating butt. All was not lost to Yuri, who knew the moment of his satisfaction was near as he exploded *with a primal scream.*

CHAPTER 9

LOUISA WAS ALREADY STARTING TO FEEL ANXIOUS AS SHE started to head north on Highway 52. A thousand questions a minute ran through her mind as she thought of what might happen when she stood face-to-face with Quinn.

Would he be home when she arrived? What if he was? What would be his first words? Her stomach churned as she neared the road to Fancy Gap at the intersection of the Blue Ridge Parkway and Highway 52.

A glance at her watch confirmed what her stomach was telling her. She was hungry. She soon pulled to a stop in the Fancy Gap Deli's parking lot. She looked around the parking lot and was relieved that Quinn's truck was not there.

Once she was certain she didn't recognize any other cars or trucks, she got out of her Volvo SUV and headed for the deli. She slowly opened the door and peeked inside. She was relieved that she didn't recognize anyone.

She sat at the far table and smiled when she saw Sharon walking toward her. Louisa stood and gave her a big hug.

"This is a surprise. Just when I was planning to put a move on that man of yours and you show up out of our Fancy Gap thin air. By golly, it's good to see you, girl. I have had the darnedest time keeping the local women's fangs out of your sweetheart. I do hope he is still your sweetheart?"

Louisa frowned and looked down at the table for a moment before she replied, "Sharon, I'm about to find out what Quinn McSpain thinks of me. I need some food in my stomach before I stand toe-to-toe with him. I've been tormented with the notion that he may just send me packing . . . and this time for good!"

Sharon reached over and took her hand. "Louisa, I have fed your man many meals in this deli since you left. My female intuition is pretty dang good, and all the vibes I get from Quinn is that he has a large hole in his life right now. Now, he is all man, and I'm sure he has tried to convince himself that he can get along quite well without you. But ya know, girlfriend, that is all poppycock. Quinn McSpain loves you and no one else.

"Heck it wasn't a bit ago that our resident Carroll County bitch Libby Thomas tried to lasso him in. Try as she may, ole Quinn kept her at bay with a stiff arm."

That brought a smile to Louisa's face as Sharon stood and looked at her. "I'm going back to the kitchen and fix up the special salad you like 'cause I don't want you to get all mushy with your man on an empty stomach."

Louisa reached for a napkin and brought it to her cheek to wipe away *a happy tear.*

———————

ANATOLY KRISTOFF STOOD OUTSIDE THE DETENTION room and took a look at the man and the woman sitting side-by-side on the bench inside. He looked at his deputy security chief sitting beside him. They had both served together in old KGB services.

"What do we know of these two?" he asked.

"Unfortunately, nothing. They do not have any form of identification. I ran their faces through our best facial recognition software to no avail. And they haven't said a word to each other since we caught them. I believe they are highly trained or just stupid."

Anatoly stood up and entered the detention room. Both Rufus and Gearleen looked at him. He sat on the bench facing them. He had two cups of coffee with him.

He smiled. "My name is Adam. I hope the men didn't hurt you in any way. Please have a cup of coffee."

Rufus reached out first, took the cup, and took a sip. Gearleen watched him and waited a moment before she took the cup in front of her. She seemed to relax a bit after she began drinking the coffee.

Anatoly smiled as he made eye contact. "Now do tell me exactly why you decided to pay us a visit today. Our visitors usually come in the front gate."

Rufus looked at Gearleen before he spoke. "Well, I'm not sure why Gearleen here needed to get closer to the fence line. Heck, I was ready to skedaddle after we saw the white van come through the gate. But, oh no . . . Gearleen here needed to get a closer look."

Gearleen punched him on the shoulder. "That is just bullcrap, Rufus. You saw some pretty women in that van and wanted to get a better look as well. Mister ole Rufus ain't as innocent as he looks."

Anatoly moved in a little closer to the table. "Does anyone know you are out here today? Your family or friends of anyone you work with?"

Rufus laughed. "Why, heck no, 'cause we don't have no children or kin that is still alive. Its just the two of us. Gearleen, did you tell anyone at the Burger King that we spend time on the ridge?"

Gearleen shook her head from side to side. "Heck no, Rufus. I don't talk to no one at work when I'm sweeping the floors or cleaning the toilets. Ain't nobody's darn business as to what we do in the woods."

Anatoly cocked his head a bit. "Did you drive over here and park somewhere close by?"

Gearleen spoke up, "Nope, we walked all the way from our cabin. And we need to be getting back 'cause we gonna miss our favorite television shows."

"Do you have cell phones?" Anatoly asked.

Rufus giggled. "Mister, no, we don't, and we don't need none either. Folks we see waste all their time on the phones. It plumb scares me when I see folks driving and pecking on those stupid phones."

Anatoly sat still for a moment before he spoke. "Folks, I must tell you that coming here was a mistake. I hope to never see you again, and I don't expect you to tell anyone about any of this. Do you understand?"

Gearleen ran her finger across her lips. "Mister, there ain't no way we will ever tell a soul 'bout any of this. Our lips are sealed!"

Anatoly stood and looked them. "Sit tight. One of my men will be right in to give you a ride home."

Both Rufus and Gearleen smiled simple smiles.

He closed the door behind him when he left. His deputy and two other men looked at him. "These two are not threats. Yet we can't take any chances. Take them to their cabin. Once you are satisfied no one else is there, you will kill them *and burn the cabin to the ground.*"

ELENA ROLLED OVER IN HER BED AND SNUCK A PEEK AT her bedside clock. Once she saw it was already nine o'clock, she quickly swung her legs out of bed and to the floor. She stood, stretched, and looked at herself in the floor-to-ceiling mirror on the other side of her room.

Just as she did, Natalia peeked in her room. "I just knew you would be late. Did you forget that Sasha is taking us out today? Are you too tired from our little visit with Yuri?"

Elena growled, "You know I like sex as much as you do but not when I'm forced to do it! That man is a pig, and we are prisoners here. Oh, I know we would be much worse off in Saint Petersburg, but at least we would be free!"

Natalia sat on her bed and laughed. "You had better be careful with what you say because they could be listening. Get in the shower and hurry up. I'm anxious to get out of here and around in this place they call Virginia."

Elena flipped her the bird as she closed the shower door. Within five minutes, she was toweled off and dressed. Natalia stood up and headed to the bedroom door.

Elena paused, went to her desk, and opened the top drawer. She took out a piece of folded paper and put it in her pocket. A smile came to her face as she followed

Natalia out of the bedroom door as they walked into the kitchen that was reserved for the girls.

Sasha glanced up from the cup of tea she was sipping. "I hope you two aren't too hungry because the more time we spend in this kitchen, the less time we have to shop."

Both girls grabbed a banana and two apples and headed to the kitchen door. Sasha took her last sip of tea and followed them. The girls were talking and giggling, as the thought of getting out to shop appealed to them both. They held hands as they followed Sasha to the garage.

Once inside, Sasha went to a large key cabinet and removed one set of keys. She walked over to a brand-new white Porsche Mecan. She opened the door for the girls, who took their seats.

Sasha slid behind the steering wheel and started it up. Within a second, one of the many garage doors started to open. Natalia was the first to comment, "This car smells so good."

"It should, ladies, as it is brand new. Nothing but the best for you two."

Natalia, who was sitting in the front seat, turned and smiled at Elena in the back seat. She giggled when Elena shot her the bird.

"Relax, you two, as we will be *in Winston-Salem in no time.*"

As Quinn drove down Lightning Ridge Road, his hands were moist holding the steering wheel. He was about to come face-to-face with the woman he loved. Yet the wedge of doubt had cast them apart for reasons only Louisa could sort out.

His mind traveled through the highlight reel of their years together. The countless hours of togetherness he had thought would never end. Yet in a moment, it came apart when a mere sliver of doubt tore open the fabric of their togetherness.

He regained his focus as he rounded the last uphill curve to his driveway. His eyes set on Louisa's Volvo parked in its usual spot. He slowed down and stopped on the crest of the driveway.

His eyes settled on Louisa sitting on the top step of the back porch. He slowly opened his truck door and stepped out. He paused for a moment before gently closing the door.

Louisa was holding her chin in her hands as he walked toward her. He stopped a foot or two before the bottom step.

Louisa looked up at him and smiled, "Do I need a reservation, or do you have room at this dump?"

Quinn tried his hardest not to laugh. "Do you mind if I sit a spell?"

Louisa patted the space next to her as he stepped to the top and sat next to her. They both looked straight ahead toward the top of Pilot Mountain in the distance.

She was the first to speak. "I think the fog just lifted before I got here."

Quinn took a few seconds before he offered, "It was thick as pea soup this morning when I left, but look at it now. It's amazing what's to be seen when the fog goes away."

Louisa took in a deep breath. "You also feel better when your fog lifts and goes away."

Quinn turned and looked at her. "And exactly when did your fog lift?"

She continued to look straight ahead and felt a tear well up. "In New Mexico, of all places. It lifted in the very moment that I realized you are the only person who means anything in my life. It lifted when I realized I was a fool who lost my mind in a foolish moment that I will regret for the rest of my life. But I was shaken to my senses with the help of another imperfect soul who spoke the truth."

Quinn cracked a smile as he looked at her. "God, Louisa, let me guess—you spent time with a priest or a bartender."

Louisa began to smile as she looked at Quinn. "Right on the second count. Her name is Hattie Bob, and she saw right through me and brought me to my senses."

Their eyes met and locked in on each other. Tears welled up in Louisa's eyes. "I am here with my heart in my hand. I screwed up royally and did the dumbest thing I've ever done in my life.

"There is no place on earth I want to be but here by your side. Nothing else matters, Quinn, not a goddamn thing! I just hope you can find it in your heart to give me a second chance."

Her left hand reached over and took his right hand. He squeezed her hand as tears rolled down his cheeks. "I have never been so alone as I am without you. Hours and hours under the stars that went silent without your breath in the night sky. Moment upon moment wondering if you would ever return. Fear gripped my heart and soul at the mere thought that you might not. I dreamed of this very moment that I would see love in your eyes."

At that moment, he turned and took her into his arms. They both sobbed uncontrollably until their lips met in a kiss.

"Don't ever let me go, Quinn McSpain! Not ever—do you hear me?"

Quinn bit the bottom of her left earlobe. "Dang, here you are for ten minutes, and you're giving orders already."

They slowly stood and embraced for the longest time.

"Louisa, you should know I've saved lots of money on wine in your absence. But not to worry—I think we can quickly drink up those savings."

Louisa backed away from him. "Well, aren't you going to invite me in?"

Quinn reached into his pocket and took out a single key. "Why don't you use this key and let us both in."

Louisa opened the door and stepped inside. She held the key out to Quinn.

"I believe that is your key, girl. I just hope you don't do anything stupid to lose it again!"

She wrapped her hand around the key and put it into her pocket. She waved one finger back and forth at him. "Don't you worry about that, big man, 'cause this little ole key is the key to my heart."

They stood toe-to-toe in the middle of the great room and were lost in their hugs and kisses. When they stopped for air, Louisa walked over to the bedroom door. She looked inside and came back to Quinn. "Now I'm really impressed. Your bed is all made up!"

Quinn reached over and picked her up in his arms. He headed to the bedroom and whispered, "Let's do something . . . *'bout that bed!*"

——◆——

RUFUS AND GEARLEEN SAT QUIETLY IN THE BACK SEAT OF the black truck they were riding in They had given directions to their cabin to the man who was driving. They were not sure if he knew where to go.

While they should have been frightened, they weren't. The men in the front seat didn't say a word. They simply looked straight ahead. Within ten minutes, the truck pulled into the long dirt road leading to the cabin.

Rufus smiled at Gearleen as the truck stopped in front of the cabin. The driver got out and pulled Rufus from the back seat. The other man opened the other door and pulled Gearleen out as well.

The first man walked up the front door of the cabin and tugged at it. Rufus spoke up, "The door is open 'cause we never lock it up." Rufus started to walk toward the front door but was stopped by the second man.

He pushed Rufus into the main room as the other man followed with Gearleen. The men looked around and had Rufus and Gearleen stand back-to-back in the middle of the room.

Both men searched the cabin and stopped when they were satisfied that no one else was in the cabin and that cameras were not set up inside the cabin. The driver took Gearleen and spun her around. Once both Rufus and Gearleen were facing each other and tied up, the second man got close to them both and said, "Remember looking at each other right now."

In a moment, he shot them both in the backs of their heads. They slumped to the cabin floor, looking at each other in their last dying moments. The driver watched them die as the other man went to their truck and returned with a five-gallon can of gasoline.

He proceeded to douse Rufus and Gearleen with gas and walked around the cabin emptying the can on their wooden furniture. Once he finished, both men walked to the cabin door. The driver stopped and took a book of matches from his pocket. He lit the first match and tossed it on the cabin floor.

Within a moment, the inside of the cabin was on fire. Gearleen felt the first flame engulf her body, as she was still alive. Rufus didn't feel a thing.

Both men sat in their truck and watched the cabin burn. They were not concerned about any fire trucks coming to the scene, as they knew the area was serviced by volunteer firefighters.

Once they were satisfied with what they saw, they turned the truck around and slowly backed out of the cabin road. Both men smiled and high-fived each other. Neither of them saw the wildlife camera that Rufus had set up toward the end of the cabin road. They never heard the camera click as it *took motion-activated pictures.*

———

SASHA DROVE THE PORSCHE MECAN DOWN HIGHWAY 52 South and turned off at Business I-40. Elena and Natalia looked out the windows as they got close to admire the Winston-Salem skyline.

She slowed the Porsche SUV when she took the Stratford Road exit. Both girls smiled as Sasha drove into the Thruway Shopping Center and slowly passed the storefronts.

Both smiled as they looked at the new boutique young women's apparel stores. Sasha stopped the car in front of the Chico's store. Both girls smiled as they jumped out of the car and headed to as many stores as they could.

The entire afternoon shopping experience lasted over three hours. The back of the Mecan was loaded with fancy bags that were full of designer dresses to stylish footwear and the very best in exotic lingerie.

Sasha smiled while she looked at the girls in the back seat as they drove north on Highway 52. It didn't take long for both of them to slump back in their seats to nap.

They awoke when the car came to a complete stop. Elena opened her eyes and realized they were parked at the Food Lion supermarket in Hillsville.

Sasha turned and smiled at them. "Come with me, as I need a few things in the market."

She opened the door and watched them get out. They stretched their long legs and followed her into the store. Several of the Food Lion male employees saw them enter as well. Several stopped in their tracks, as they had never laid eyes on two more beautiful women. The older store manager fixed his eyes on Sasha as she walked down the aisles behind her cart.

Deputy Sue Ann Kollman had just finished her shift and stopped in the Food Lion to pick up some beer and wine. She was still in her uniform as she walked down the long aisle by the meat section when Elena caught sight of her.

That caught her by surprise, as she suddenly remembered that she had the note she'd written in her pocket. She put her hand in her pocket and put the note between her fingers.

Sasha was walking directly toward the deputy with Elena and Natalia behind her. Sasha smiled at Kollman as she slowly walked by. Kollman didn't pay much attention until she looked at both of the girls. She was immediately taken by their beauty.

She thought that the taller of the two girls had made eye contact with her. As they came within a foot of her, the taller girl quickly thrust out her hand and put a piece of folded paper in her hand.

The tall girl then quickly put one finger to her lips as they passed and continued down the aisle. Deputy Kollman watched them walk down the aisle before she unfolded the note.

She read the words slowly before she muttered, "*Oh, shit!*"

———

THE REPORT OF A CABIN OF FIRE IN PIPERS GAP CAME into the Twin County E-911 Regional Dispatch Center from someone at the Felts Garage. The fire department in Hillsville dispatched a truck and EMS rescue squad. The caller didn't know the exact location of the fire.

The driver of the fire truck sped down from the top of Pipers Gap Road. Stan Surratt, who sat beside him, was first to spot the smoke. They quickly turned down the old logging road on their left and drove for two and a half miles.

Surratt spotted the narrow dirt road that led to Rufus and Gearleen's cabin. The fire truck came to a stop some fifty feet from the burned-out cabin. Both men jumped out and activated a water line from the pumper.

Within five minutes, they stopped spraying water, as the fire had leveled the cabin. By that time, the EMS ambulance team arrived at the cabin.

Tyler Shelor, the senior EMS lead, walked over and looked at Surratt. "Dang, Stan, you think anyone was in there when it burned?"

Surratt shook his head. "Let's take a look. Someone might have been in there, and we won't know till we look."

It didn't take them long to stop in their tracks as they looked around the charred interior of the cabin. Surratt pointed down to what looked like two burned corpses lying in front of them.

Shelor spoke first, "Stan, those are two barbecued bodies, my friend. But I wonder who they are. Do you have any notion as to who lived here?"

Surratt shook his head from side to side. "I don't, Tyler, but we better get back outside and call the sheriff 'cause this is a crime scene."

Shelor shook his head. "*Sure nuff is!*"

CHAPTER 10

THE PRESIDENT'S CHIEF OF STAFF, FRANK STILLHOUSE, looked out of his office and smiled. His day had been horrific. The president wanted to fire the White House press secretary but cooled his burners when Stillhouse talked him out of it.

Craig Rogers had been elected president because of his fiery personality and his willingness to buck the system and make massive changes to the way Washington worked. Frank Stillhouse worked very hard to keep him out of political quicksand.

This was his Thursday to savor, as the president was traveling to Europe for a week and would be out of his hair. He had advised the president that he would be taking a few days off to visit some friends in southwest Virginia.

His private phone rang, and he saw the name of his best friend displayed at the top. "Well, Dan Nelson, I hope your day has been better than mine, and I hope you have good news about the upcoming weekend."

Nelson was a billionaire industrialist who had served in Vietnam with Stillhouse and had saved his life in a treacherous firefight during the war. To this day, they were the closest of friends.

"You know darn well that I had a great day 'cause you know what the stock market did today. Now I only wish I could be going with you on your little sojourn this weekend. But I just can't get out of the trip to California."

Stillhouse smiled at his friend's comment. Nelson had set up Stillhouse's weekend trip to the retreat in southwest Virginia. He was also paying the $50,000 tab associated with his friend's visit to the retreat.

While he knew through his Russian contact what his friend would enjoy at the retreat, few others were privileged with that information. His payment was made through bitcoins and was untraceable.

He also knew that Stillhouse's wife was off to a girls' weekend in Colorado. Thus, it was a perfect time for his friend's sexual escapade. He also knew through reliable sources that Phyllis Stillhouse was meeting her lover in the Colorado Rockies.

His friend was deeply in love with Phyllis and would never imagine that she was cheating on him. Yet he knew that Phyllis was really only interested in the sex and harbored no true affection for her lover.

"So, listen, Frank, this is the plan. You drive to my place in Falls Church right after lunch tomorrow. Don't get there later than one in the afternoon, as a helicopter will pick you up at my landing pad in the back of the house. There will be a pilot and another man flying with him. The helicopter will have a blue cross painted on the side. The trip will take approximately an hour and a half. The pilot and the man with him will not talk to you.

"Once you land at the compound, another man will greet you. His name is Yuri. He will be your guide and only contact for the twenty-four hours you will be on the ground. Yuri is a man you can trust."

Stillhouse listened attentively. "Pray tell, exactly what can I expect in those twenty-four hours? You really haven't clued me in on the details, buddy."

Nelson chuckled. "My friend, I know that your bride has never been one to raise your blood pressure with her sexual prowess. And I know from all of our years together that your sexual fantasies are . . . well, unfulfilled. So, in the twenty-four hours you spend at the retreat, you will be taken to places even you have never dreamed of."

There was a pause on the other end of the line. "If it's gonna be all that good, why aren't you coming along?"

"Buddy, you will be the only guest in the house. I couldn't go even if I wanted to go with you. But I will meet you at my place when you return, and I will expect a full briefing."

"Good gracious, Dan, I'm getting all hot and bothered with my imagination going hog wild. How much do I owe you for this little trip to engage all of my sexual fantasies?"

"Brother, not one red cent. This treat is all on me. I have never forgotten what you did for me such a long time ago and what you continue to do for me through your sway with certain government agencies. That has been very helpful and profitable.

"Now listen to this: remember to pack your Cialis, and please don't *fall in love!*"

———

SUE ANN KOLLMAN READ THE NOTE IN HER HANDS A second time: "Please help us. We are being held captive!" She looked up again at the three women who were now out of the checkout line and walking to the parking lot.

She left her cart where it was and slowly walked over to the plate glass window that faced the parking lot. She saw all three women as they approached an expensive-looking car.

The notion that two of the girls were young and very pretty was not lost on her. The older woman with them was beautiful as well. The fact that they were all well dressed in expensive clothes was sinking in.

As soon as their car started to move out of the parking lot, Kollman walked quickly to her own truck. She was pleased that she wasn't driving a patrol car from the sheriff's department. Her ten-year-old Ford 150 wouldn't stand out.

The Porsche turned left and headed south on Highway 52. She was too far away to see what numbers were on the license plate. Yet she was fairly sure it was a Virginia tag.

The car was traveling right at fifty-five miles an hour until it approached Fancy Gap. The driver turned the right blinker on, signaling a turn onto the Blue Ridge Parkway after it passed the Gulf gas station.

Kollman slowed down before taking the right-hand turn off of Highway 52. She watched the Porsche take a right onto the Blue Ridge Parkway. That concerned her, as she knew it would be harder to follow the Porsche on the parkway since there would be fewer cars and trucks there.

As she drove, Kollman couldn't yet wrap her mind around exactly what was going on in front of her. She re-read the note as she drove and tried to imagine possible situations where a beautiful, well-dressed young woman being driven around in an expensive car was being held against her will.

She had traveled a good twenty-five miles and had lost sight of the Porsche. As she rounded a curve and passed over Pipers Gap Road Bridge, she caught sight of the Porsche already on Pipers Gap Road.

With a quick twist of her steering wheel as she pumped her brakes, she managed to take the right turn that would take her to Pipers Gap Road. As she straightened her truck out, she sped up, as she knew the road well and realized she might miss the Porsche if it sped up or turned off.

Within five minutes, she rounded a curve and saw the brake lights on the Porsche turn red at it slowed to take a left-hand turn. Kollman jammed on her brakes and skidded to a stop. As soon as she caught her breath, she slowly turned left and drove slowly along the narrow road.

Within a half mile, she saw the Porsche slow down and turn onto the road that led to the religious compound. She knew the main gate was some two hundred yards ahead.

She pulled her truck onto the side of the road and ran up the road until she could see the gate. The massive gates were opened, and the Porsche drove on through. Kollman stood there for a moment before she walked back to her truck.

She closed the door and sat in silence for a moment before she picked the note and read it again. She shook her head as she muttered, "*What the fuck is that all about?*"

———◆———

LEVI BLACKBURN HAD JUST FINISHED TYPING A REPORT when his cell phone buzzed. He loved investigating criminal activity and especially putting bad people in jail. But what he despised was typing reports.

He looked down at his phone and saw Stan Surratt's name on the screen. He knew Surratt from their days in grammar school together. He also respected the fine work Surratt had done as a first responder on the county EMS team.

"Stan, I know this ain't no social call at this time of day. My day's 'bout over, so don't tell me nothing to screw that up, buddy!"

Levi heard laughter on the other end. "There is nothing I like better than making you work late. We all know you are the biggest slacker in the Carroll County Sheriff's Department. Folks here in EMS take bets on when the sheriff gives you your walking papers."

"Listen, buddy, you better wish I never leave this department 'cause if I do, who else will solve all of the high-profile criminal activity in the county?"

"Cowboy, what I need for you to do is jump in the truck of yours and skedaddle out of Hillsville and meet me on Pipers Gap 'cause it looks like two folks got burned to a crisp in a cabin fire out here."

Levi paused for a moment before replying, "Let me guess—in your professional opinion, it wasn't an accident either?"

"Sure nuff, Brother Blackburn. I believe these two folks were tied up and burned to death. But you do need to see this."

"Send me a message with the address and directions, and I'll be there in fifteen minutes."

Levi searched the county database for an address check. When Rufus's and Gearleen's names came across the screen, he could not associate those names with anyone he knew.

He thought that was puzzling as he drove toward Pipers Gap. He either knew or had heard of most folks in Carroll County. Since only some thirty-three thousand residents lived in the county, he had heard of or come into contact with most of them over the course of the years he had lived there.

He soon turned off the Blue Ridge Parkway and headed down Pipers Gap Road. He slowed to take the left turn Stan had suggested he take. Within a mile and a half, he saw the county EMS truck parked at the entrance to a small dirt road.

As Levi pulled in beside it, Stan Surratt got out to greet him. "I'm impressed, Levi Blackburn, 'cause you seem to have found us all by yourself."

Levi chuckled and then embraced his friend. "God, you stink like smoke, Stan. Your ole lady ain't gonna like that when you get home, brother. Now why in the dickens did you have me come out to this piece of nowhere?"

"Follow me, turkey, 'cause you gonna earn your pay for a change," Surratt offered as he led the way down the dirt road.

Levi followed behind him as the road narrowed and the smell of old smoke filled the air. Surratt stopped just short of what remained of the cabin.

"Dang, Stan, looks like somebody had a barbeque here, brother," Levi offered as he slipped on rubber gloves. He moved around the perimeter of what remained of the cabin and worked his way inward. He stopped in the middle of the floor and looked down at what looked like the remains of two charred bodies. Levi squatted down as he looked at the pile of burned flesh in front of him. He shook his head from side to side as he looked up at Surratt. "Stan, it does look like ole Rufus and Gearleen were murdered, my friend. Sure nuff does."

It appeared as though one body was lying over the other on the floor of the cabin. "Stan, I'll bet you a case of Bud Light that ole Rufus crawled over Gearleen in order to protect her from the flames."

Levi moved what looked like the bigger of the two skulls over on its side. He pointed to a small hole in the back of the skull. "Stan, look at this. These two were shot before the fire was started. Whoever did this wanted to cover their tracks as best they could."

Surratt shook his head. "Levi, what do you know of these two folks? I didn't even know this cabin existed."

"You and me both, brother. I've got to do some digging to find out as much as I can about these two and why in the world someone wanted them dead. This looks like an execution-style killing done by professionals. And that puzzles me to no end. Without knowing these two, I'll go out on a limb and speculate that they, like most folks in Carroll County, weren't exactly rich in any way, shape, or form. Hell, look around this place and just imagine what they didn't have!

"I'm gonna call the crime scene folks at the state police in Wytheville and get them out here to take a look at all of this. There might be some evidence to be found, but I really doubt it."

Surratt followed Levi out of the cabin, back to the road. He watched Levi look from side to side as he slowly walked back to their vehicles.

Just before getting back to the edge of the road, Levi stopped in his tracks. He took five steps into the brush, where he looked closely at a small pine tree. Surratt strained to see what Levi was looking at. Levi reached into his pocket and took out his jackknife. With one swipe, he cut the small band that was holding the object to the tree.

He turned and held the object up for Surratt to see.

"I'll be dipped," Surratt offered as he looked at the motion-activated field wildlife camera Levi was holding.

Levi smiled as he examined the camera housing. "Lookie here, Stan! Look what ole Levi found himself!"

Surratt smiled. "Dang, Levi, you better at this than I thought you be! And that camera looks to be in pretty good shape. Hell, much better that most of mine are!"

Levi smiled. "I'm gonna bet that the batteries in this ole camera are working and the memory card is in good shape. And if they are, I'm gonna put the motherfuckers who killed these two in jail . . . *for a long time!*"

FRANK STILLHOUSE PARKED HIS RANGE ROVER AT THE location he was told the helicopter would land to pick him up. He checked his watch and was pleased that he was ten minutes early.

He thought of the description his friend Dan Nelson had passed along about what the next twenty-four hours might hold for him. His imagination started to go in a hundred different directions with what sexual escapades might lie in store for him.

While he loved his wife and was truly indebted to her for her unyielding support during his political career, he understood that she had slowly lost her desire for any type of sexual encounter.

He suspected that she might expect him to gain some sort of sexual satisfaction from other women in his life. He also understood that she expected him to be discreet.

The endless possibilities of sexual delights continued to float through his mind only to be interrupted by the sight of a helicopter landing some one hundred yards from where he was parked.

He watched the gleaming stainless-steel helicopter land before he left his vehicle and walked over toward it. He saw the pilot and another man seated inside the helicopter.

As he approached, the side door opened, and a tall man emerged. He held out his hand and offered, "Welcome aboard, sir!" He quickly turned, opened the back door of the helicopter, and motioned Stillhouse to step in.

Once inside, he slipped to the inner seat as the tall man sat in front of him, near the pilot. It took him a moment to realize there was another person on board. He tuned to his right to see a woman moving from the third row to sit next to him.

He was immediately taken by her striking beauty. She smiled at him and reached over to pick up two champagne flutes, which she set down on the small table between them. She opened the small refrigerator beside her and removed a bottle of champagne.

Stillhouse immediately recognized the bottle as a very expensive and rare French offering. She slowly removed the cork as the helicopter slowly left the ground. Within a moment, she handed the flute to him. She lifted hers and smiled as she reached over and touched his glass with hers.

He admired her long, golden-blond hair and her perfect smile. She was wearing a short velvet sport coat and tight-fitting tan shorts. Her long, perfect, bare legs were crossed, and the sight of her red stiletto heels excited him.

Just as he began to ask her name, she dipped her right forefinger in her champagne and slowly brought it to her lips. Her tongue licked the droplets of champagne from her finger.

Stillhouse suddenly felt surges of arousal. She slid slightly closer to him and dipped her finger into his flute. He watched her finger as she brought it to his lips. He opened his mouth and slowly licked her finger with his tongue.

His heartbeat quickened as she took another sip of champagne. He looked into her blue eyes but soon followed her free hand, which began to unbutton her velvet sport coat.

He was mesmerized at what was playing out no more than two feet from his seat. She slowly worked her way down to the last of four buttons and let the coat open at the middle.

Stillhouse tensed up as she reached for his free hand. She brought his hand to her lips and proceeded to slowly lick all his fingers. That brought a sudden rush of blood to his manhood.

While his fingers were still moist, she lowered his hand to her navel and rubbed it along the skin below her belly button. He tried to relax as she worked his hand up her ribcage to the base of her breasts.

He licked his lips as she lifted his open palm to her left breast. He closed his eyes, and the arousal of the moment began to intensify. He felt the firm mound of her velvety soft breast as she guided his hand to the other side.

By this time, he felt his manhood stiffen and start to feel uncomfortable in his slacks. As she set his hand down, she slowly slipped the coat from her shoulders.

Stillhouse admired her perfect torso; she smiled and inched even closer to him. She noticed his discomfort as she undid the top button of his trousers. He groaned a sigh of relief when she lowered the zipper.

She slipped her hands under his buttocks and slowly pulled his trousers down to his ankles. He watched her hands slide up his legs and stop just short of his briefs.

He marveled at how erect he had become. He groaned as she licked the top part of his briefs and nibbled at his manhood underneath. His senses began to twirl as she looped her fingers into the top of his briefs and pulled them down.

His erection stood firm and tall as she blew warm air along the shaft and started to lick from top to bottom. His eyes closed; she opened her mouth and smiled at him.

Stillhouse lost track of time as she worked her magic on his manhood. He was doing his best to hold himself back from responding too quickly to the moment. His resolve weakened while her sensual and fluid movements brought him to the brink.

His explosion came without warning. He felt the spasms jolt through his whole body. He slowly opened his eyes to see her licking her lips and smiling. That brought a smile to his face as he closed his eyes and only wished he could have seen what just happened.

What he didn't see was the small pinhole camera that was recording all that had just happened . . . *for posterity.*

CHAPTER 11

LOUISA SLOWLY OPENED ONE EYE AND THEN THE OTHER. She rolled over and looked at Quinn, who was still sound asleep. She turned to her other side to see the first light of the day peeking over the eastern ridge.

A broad smile came to her face as she silently swung her legs off the bed to the floor. The floor gave off a few squeaks as she tiptoed out of the bedroom, gently closing the door behind her.

A glimpse in the hall mirror suggested that she'd forgotten her robe in the bedroom. That was remedied as she took Quinn's flannel shirt that was hanging on a kitchen chair.

His smell overwhelmed her as she took the French press out and measured the coffee grounds. She looked out the north window and poured hot water into the press.

Birds were flying about as the hummingbirds took turns at the feeder. Within a moment, with the French press and her cup in hand, she headed to the eastern side of the deck.

The morning sun was just peeking above the trees. She set the press down after she filled her cup to the brim. Once she settled into her favorite rocking chair, she put her lips to the cup.

With that first sip came a tiny teardrop that settled on her cheek. Her mind reminded her of how lucky she was to be back in Fancy Gap. She shuddered at the thought that she could have been banished from Quinn's life forever.

She wiped away the tear as two barn swallows circled overhead and chirped sounds that were music to her ears. Her mind's eye floated through what had happened in the last month. A promise developed in the deep recesses of her mind to erase all those negative moments.

Hattie Bob's words resonated between her ears as she reminded herself to send a note of thanks to that wonderful woman in New Mexico.

Louisa didn't hear Quinn come up behind her. "Really didn't know when I might see this chair filled again," he offered. He took a long sip of his coffee and smiled while he looked at her.

Louisa's eyes locked on to his as she took another sip. "McSpain, nothing—and I mean nothing—will ever get me out of this chair again! My life if too short to waste precious moments not being near the man I love. I was a fool, and I admit it. But not to worry because I will never be a fool again!"

Quinn took a long sip. "Then I suppose since you are . . . or were a good Catholic and you seem to be begging my forgiveness, I guess three Our Fathers and three Hail Marys just might get you back in my good graces. Oh, wait, one more thing . . . and some tender loving will seal the deal!"

Louisa almost spit out her last sip. She offered a coy smile. "Pray tell, were you a celibate altar boy while I was away? I just know that Libby must have tried to get her fangs in you!"

Quinn looked away, trying hard not to giggle. "The truth is I had to hire one of Leroy's off-duty deputies to control traffic. The line of aspiring lovelies came from as far as Roanoke in Virginia to Raleigh in North Carolina. Levi even tried to sell admission tickets. Some sent flowers, but unfortunately, none of them had the good sense to lure me into their arms with wine."

Louisa couldn't control her laughter. She smiled as she stood in front of Quinn and removed the shirt she was wearing. "Are you ready for your breakfast now?"

Quinn stood and spoke as he let his robe fall to the deck. *"I'll have you, sunny side up."*

———

VLADIMIR PUTIN SMILED AFTER HIS MONDAY STAFF MEETing had finished. He was pleased with the majority of large-scale projects his team had initiated around the world. He was especially pleased with the meeting he'd had with President Rogers in Helsinki.

The outrage in the United States was far greater than he could have hoped for. He was almost certain that Rogers was going to invite him to Washington.

Anton Laino, his chief of staff, was the one person left in the room.

"Anton, please do tell me you have good news from our brothers in the Bratva. I know they have been working on the assignment I commissioned several months ago."

"Vladimir, you will be pleased, as the tree we planted will soon begin to bear fruit. It seems that my counterpart Frank Stillhouse in the Rogers inner circle decided to taste a bit of the forbidden fruit. In the next day or so, he will engage his sexual fantasies with the seven beautiful young ladies who have been trained for this very task. We will have a complete video library of all his moments in the twenty-four hours he spends in our little spider's nest."

Putin smiled as he stood and patted Laino on the back. "That, my friend, will give us the most leverage we could have ever hoped for! *He truly will be screwed!*"

———

LEVI SAT AT HIS DESK AND LOOKED AT THE WILDLIFE camera he had recovered from the cabin. The outer case was secured with a small lock. While he didn't have the key to the lock, he knew how he could open it.

He walked over to the small supply cabinet at the other end of the room. Once inside, he quickly found what he was looking for. He hadn't used these bolt cutters in quite some time.

As he walked back to his desk, the sheriff came out of his office. "Okay, Levi, let me guess—your girlfriend locked her chastity belt and you can't find the key."

"Well, now, now, Sheriff, aren't you just a funny one. But never you worry—ole Levi here would never have to worry bout no such thing. No sirree—not ole Levi here!"

"Then do share with me what you need those bolt cutters for."

Levi motioned to the sheriff to follow him back to his desk. "Leroy, this here camera probably has some pictures of the idiots who killed that couple up at Pipers Gap. All I need to do is cut the lock off and hope the batteries inside are fresh and the camera worked as it should have."

Levi sat and quickly snapped the lock off. He opened the camera and jumped back a bit as a small spider came out and landed on his desk. "Kill that damn thing, Sheriff!" Levi blurted out.

Leroy took one swat and flattened the spider in its tracks. "I didn't know you were afraid of spiders, Levi."

"Jeez, Leroy, there just ain't much I'm afraid of, but those damn creepy spiders are at the top of the list. Got bit real bad when I was a kid, and I got real sick. Bit me on the ass when I was in bed. Left a bad scar, and I can show you that, Leroy!"

"That won't be necessary, Levi. I'll take your word on that. Let's see what is on that card."

Levi pulled the inner panel open and removed the SD card. "This looks okay, and it's a high capacity card," Levi offered as he inserted the card in the slot on his laptop.

After a few keystrokes, images began to appear on the screen. The very first were of deer and wild turkeys who were in range of the camera and activated it. Levi stopped when the frame on the screen showed a man and a woman waving at the camera.

"I be dipped—that must be the Rufus and Gearleen who lived at the cabin. It looks like that picture wasn't taken too long ago, Sheriff."

"Tell me, Levi, exactly who were Rufus and Gearleen?" Leroy asked.

"Well, Sheriff, those two were—now, what is the word I'm looking for? Oh, now I got it—they were recluse types. I understand he cut grass for folks from time to time, and I guess she worked part time at the Burger King here in Hillsville. But for the most part, they stuck to themselves. So, I'm having to think hard 'bout what they might have seen or done to have somebody burn them to death."

The sheriff scratched his chin. "I agree, Levi, there has to be more to this that we need to discover. So, keep clicking those images so we might see exactly who might be responsible for their deaths."

Levi went through at least thirty frames before he suddenly stopped. "Well, dang, Leroy . . . *now what have we got here?*"

FRANK STILLHOUSE WAS STILL SMILING WHEN THE WOMAN slipped the silk hood over his head. She assured him it wouldn't be on for long. She took his right hand and massaged both of her breasts as the helicopter started to descend.

Once it landed, she took the hood off his face. As his eyes adjusted, he saw a man standing some one hundred feet from the landing pad. The man was surrounded by at least seven women.

Once the helicopter was completely still, the man, who was dressed in a white shirt, walked toward the landing pad. He opened the door and smiled as Frank stepped out. "Frank, welcome to our happy place. My name is Yuri, and I hope you enjoyed the short trip to our little piece of heaven."

Frank smiled. "That truly was first-class service. I can only hope the return trip is as enjoyable!"

Yuri led him off of the landing pad toward the seven women, who were all smiling. He stopped at the first girl. "Frank, this is Elena, and she will be the first to show you around."

Elena stepped forward and gave him a kiss on the cheek. As Yuri introduced him to the six other girls, Frank was flabbergasted with the pristine and angelic beauty of each of the girls.

After the introductions, Yuri and Frank walked toward the main building. Frank noticed the tall white cross which dominated the landscape. "Yuri, I'm sorry, but I have to ask, why the cross?"

Yuri smiled. "In the next twenty-four hours, you will come to see this as . . . *a sacred experience.*"

LOUISA WATCHED QUINN DO THE BREAKFAST DISHES AF-
ter they ate. She loved that man beyond what she ever
thought herself capable of. Her head shook ever so
slightly from side to side at the notion that she had
been on the brink of losing him forever.

Quinn realized she was lost in thought as he threw
the dish towel toward her. "So, we made passionate love
and I fed you, and it's not quite nine o'clock yet. I know
you must be exhausted from our little tete-a-tete on the
porch, but how about a nice little bike ride?"

Louisa lit up in a moment. "Now you're talking, big
fella. Its been a while since I've been in the saddle, but
not a problem 'cause I know I can still make you cry
uncle."

"Dream on, Hawke! I'm going to pack a tow rope
that we'll need to tow you back to the house."

Louisa brushed her teeth and slipped into her bik-
ing tights and sports bra. She would never admit that
she was a bit worried that Quinn might push her way
beyond where she would like to be.

Within fifteen minutes, they were on the Blue Ridge
Parkway heading toward Meadows of Dan. As they ap-
proached the first major uphill after Orchard Gap Road,
Louisa decided to push the pace up the hill.

Nearing the top, she felt Quinn right on her
rear wheel. He stayed there until they got closer to
Groundhog Mountain, where he lifted up out of the

saddle and flew by Louisa. Caught a bit by surprise, she quickly recovered and slowed as they turned into the parking lot at the top.

Quinn swung off his bike and took out his water bottle before sitting on the curb. Louisa was somewhat befuddled by all of this. She rested her bike against a tree and sat next to him.

"Okay, I hope I didn't zap too much of your energy this morning before breakfast?" she asked.

Quinn smiled as he looked at her. "Louisa, there is something strange happening with my endurance. This isn't the first time I've felt tired after a minimal amount of exercise. I rode a thirty-miler the other day, and I was wiped out after the ride. So, I'm thinking, I'm getting old and this might be a natural progression. But all of this is too sudden. Heck, a month ago I rode seventy-five miles through these hills and was hardly winded."

Louisa looked at him. "When was your last physical? I don't think you've had one in two years. Is that right?"

Quinn took a sip of water and wiped the sweat off his brow. "That is about right. It's been at least two years."

Louisa stood. "Okay, that settles it. We'll make an appointment just as soon as we get back to the house. That is if you can make it back to the house?"

Quinn took another sip of water and swung his leg onto his bike. In one fell swoop, he started pedaling out of the parking lot back toward the Blue Ridge Parkway. He cocked his head a bit, as he thought he heard Louisa *laughing*.

———

THE SHERIFF AND LEVI LOOKED AT SEVERAL FRAMES ON his laptop screen. "Dang, Leroy, that sure is a black Ford 150 pickup with an extended cab. Now if only we could see the whole license plate." Levi pivoted the picture on the screen. "It's a Virginia tag for sure, but what are the numbers and letters?" He reached into his desk and took out a magnifying glass. He scanned several of the frames and scribbled notes on his desk calendar. After a minute or so, he stopped. "My bet is that we are looking at ALE-1918. I'm not 100 percent sure of this, but I think it's close."

Levi closed that screen and opened another. He quickly typed in the plate letters and numbers. Within a second or two, the screen lit up with the description of the vehicle registered to that tag.

Leroy and Levi read the page together and then looked at each other. Levi was the first to speak. "Jeez, Leroy, this suggests that the black truck belongs to the church group that built that big conference center in Pipers Gap. Crap, I wonder if someone stole their truck?"

The sheriff continued to look at the screen. "That is a possibility, Levi, but why don't you discreetly look into all of this and see what shakes out."

"Leroy, I will be all over this like a fly on shit, but not to worry, I will be discreet . . . *at least for a while.*"

———

Yuri led Frank Stillhouse into a grotto-like room filled with pools and waterfalls. Elena was close behind. Once inside, Yuri smiled as he put Frank's hand in Elena's. "Now, my friend, is the moment your fantasies come to life. I leave you with Elena and will see you after your journey is complete," he offered before leaving the grotto.

Without saying a word, Elena sat Frank down in a velvet, throne-like chair. She smiled as she spoke, "There will be nothing better than a warm bath after your journey today."

Frank didn't reply as she knelt before him and slid his loafers off. With delicate motions, she slipped each of his cashmere socks off. She then held his left foot high and started to kiss and massage his foot.

Her effort began to excite him. That increased as she slipped off her blouse and rubbed his foot in a circle around her firm and ample breast. Frank was taken with her stunning adolescent beauty. He could not think of another woman who was as beautiful.

As she finished with his feet, she took his hand and had him stand. She loosened and removed his belt. His trousers did not fall free, as his erection prevented them from falling.

With tender hands, Elena carefully lowered his trousers to the floor. She then led him to teacup-shaped half bathtub that was already half full of warm water. Frank reclined in the water and felt jets activate under his back and buttocks.

Elena slowly slid out of her shorts and stood in front of him. He again marveled at her perfection. In a moment, she knelt beside him and slowly started to lather his body. He started to breathe heavily as she caressed his belly and gently stroked his erection.

Frank closed his eyes as his level of arousal rose. He opened his eyes as he felt another presence in the room. Natalia slowly walked into the room wearing a flowing white silk robe. Frank was mesmerized by her movements.

She stood by Elena and began to passionately kiss her. As she stopped, she let her robe fall to the floor. She then slowly stepped into the tub and stood over Frank. She massaged her body as she lowered herself closer and closer to his lips.

Frank licked his lips and tried to lick her. Yet she playfully pulled away as he got closer. In a moment, Elena put one hand behind his head, her other behind Natalia's buttocks, and moved them together until they met.

Frank tasted the sweetness of her nectar as she undulated in his face. Elena engulfed his manhood and rhythmically enhanced his pleasure. She suddenly stopped, as she sensed he was about to explode.

Natalia pulled away at the same moment. Frank looked bewildered as he smiled. Elena leaned over and whispered in his ear, "Not yet—*we have only just begun.*"

QUINN WALKED OUT OF THE SHOWER AND STARTED TO towel off. He was exhausted after the ride. His effort to beat Louisa back to his house had taken a toll. Yet he was trying his best not to let on as to how tired he really was.

Louisa was in the living room and walked toward the bedroom. "Okay, my dearest, let's not put off what we can accomplish right away. Pick up that phone and make an appointment with Doctor John."

Quinn slipped on his t-shirt and laughed. "Aren't you full of yourself? Back just a short time and already barking out orders. What's a guy to do?"

"What you're going to do, big man, is pick up the phone right now and make the call. No if, ands, or buts about it! Or I'll call for you!"

Quinn smiled as he went over to the kitchen table and picked up his cell phone. He punched in a speed dial number. On the second ring, a person answered the call.

"John, it really is me calling. I know it's been like forever since I saw you, but my sweetheart Louisa here thinks I should see you and see you soon."

Quinn paused as he listened. "I guess it must be my lucky day. I'll see you in two hours." After he hung up, he snickered at Louisa. "Well, there I went and did it, but you can't come!"

"Dream on, McSpain. I'm not only going . . . *I'm driving*!"

CHAPTER 12

SUE ANN KOLLMAN STEPPED OUT OF THE SHOWER AND grabbed the towel hanging on the door. While the shower felt good, she was still preoccupied with the note the young woman had passed to her in the Food Lion.

After she was toweled off, she stood still as she looked at herself in the full-length mirror. A smirk crossed her face as her mind drifted back to the last time she'd stood there with Tommie Cruz.

He used her, and she knew it. But it didn't matter at all. She knew that he was sexually involved with another woman in Galax, but that didn't matter either. What she did know was that when he was with her, he made her feel like the most beautiful woman on earth.

She had shivered and started to cry when his life had ended and at hands of Levi Blackburn and Quinn McSpain. The pain of his death was like a dagger through her heart. That hole still leaked the blood of her remorse, which wouldn't go away.

Once she was dressed, she sat at her kitchen table and looked at the note again. While she knew that the Russian Mafia was behind the faked Christian conference center in Pipers Gap, she didn't know what was happening inside the compound.

Tommie had given her bits and pieces of information about the operation, as he was instrumental in setting up their entire information and communication infrastructure. She certainly would have been privy to more if he hadn't lost his life.

Tommie did, however, tell her to call a certain cell number and ask for Yuri if she was ever in trouble and needed any kind of protection. She powered up her iPhone and looked up the number.

She stared at the number for the longest time before she hit the call button. It rang several times before a voice answered. "Hello . . . who is this?"

Sue Ann swallowed. "Is this Yuri?" she asked.

"And exactly who is asking?" the voice replied.

"This is Sue Ann, and I was given this number by my friend Tommie Cruz."

"Ah, yes, indeed. I wondered if you would ever call, Ms. Sue Ann Kollman. I knew that Tommie had given my name to you with the instructions to call if you needed help at any time. Are you still working at the sheriff's department?"

"Yes, I am," she replied.

"So, to what do I owe the pleasure of this call? Are you in trouble?" he asked.

"Oh, no, I'm not, but this is something I think you need to know. So, after my shift yesterday, I went to the Food Lion in Hillsville to pick up a few things. While I was there, I noticed two beautiful young ladies accompanied by an attractive older woman. Trust me, these women caught my attention because I immediately knew they just didn't fit in roaming the aisles of our Food Lion. Maybe at one of those fancy stores in Winston-Salem, but not in our neck of the woods. They just stood out like sore thumbs in that supermarket. The old coots and young men working there couldn't keep their eyes off of them.

"I kind of ignored them until one of the young ladies deliberately bumped into me and passed a note into the palm of my hand. I didn't read it until I left the market and sat in my truck. As I read it for the third time, I saw them walk out of the Food Lion and get into a Porsche SUV. That also struck me as strange, as I had never seen that SUV on any of our Carroll County highways and byways.

"As they drove out of the parking lot, I decided to follow them. They drove south on Highway 52 until they reached the Blue Ridge Parkway in Fancy Gap. They turned onto the parkway and headed toward Pipers Gap.

"I knew I was far enough behind them so they wouldn't spot me tailing them. After they turned off the parkway down Pipers Gap Road, they eventually headed right to the main gate of your compound. They waved to the security staff as they drove through."

Once Yuri was satisfied that she was through talking, he offered, "Wow, Sue Ann, that is very interesting. I knew that some of our staff were out and about, but I thought they were in Winston-Salem. So, did the girls look distressed in the supermarket?" he asked.

"No, not at all. As matter of fact, I thought they acted like young teenage girls who were on a field trip. They just seemed happy."

Yuri paused for a moment before he spoke, "Okay, then, what I need is for you to bring me the note. Can you come by the day after tomorrow?"

"Sure I can. That will work, as it's my day off."

"Good. Can you be here in the afternoon?"

"That will work. Don't you want to know what the note says or which of the young ladies gave it to me?"

"Sue Ann, I am a very patient man. I'm certain not much will change on this end before I see you in two days. And we will have more time to digest the facts and properly identify the young lady in question. Are you good with this, Sue Ann?"

"I am good with that, and understand that I'm doing this because Tommie liked working with you. I also know that you paid him rather well for what he did for you."

"That is nice of you, Sue Ann. But please bear in mind that we are capable of paying you a lot of money if you can work with us. Tommie passed along that the Mexican drug lords paid you a nice amount for information you gave them from the sheriff's department."

Sue Ann was taken back by his comment. "I will be happy to discuss possibilities when we meet. I look forward to seeing you soon," she offered before she hung up.

Her mind raced backward as she thought, *Now what else did Tommie tell them?*

———————

FRANK STILLHOUSE HELD ELENA'S AND NATALIA'S hands as they led him into another chamber. Soft light bathed a small room with a high circular bed in the middle. Frank giggled like a small child as he realized that he and the two women he was with were naked.

Both girls helped him to the center of the bed. They smiled as they extended his arms behind him and wrapped his wrists with small satin ropes. Once they tied off the ends to the harnesses behind the bed, they slid down the bed beside him and caressed every inch of his body until they arrived at his ankles.

Each took hold of his legs and spread them apart. They slowly wrapped his ankles as well and secured them to harnesses at the foot of the bed. Frank could not take his eyes off of them as they stood and both leaned over to kiss him.

No sooner had they finished a door to the side of the room opened and two young women entered the room. Both were dressed as French maids. Elena took both of them to the side of the bed.

"I hope we took good care, but I'm certain that Inga and Veronika will satisfy your every dream." Elena and Natalia then kissed him as well as the other two girls before they left the room.

Frank was taken by the beauty of the new girls who entered the room. Inga bent over and whispered in his ear, "you will soon forget of those two. I promise!"

Frank's eyes rolled, as he could only imagine what was in store for him. Both girls picked up long rods with feathers on the sides and ends. Within a moment, Frank began to feel his excitement rise as the girls tickled every each of his body. He moaned loudly *as the girls worked their magic.*

DEEP INSIDE THE KREMLIN'S SENATE BUILDING, SEVERAL people walked into the office of the Russian president.

Vladimir Putin looked and motioned for the men to sit down. Sergei Ivanov looked at Anton Laino who was smiling.

Putin finished what he was doing and looked at Ivanov. "So, Sergei, what have you brought me?"

Ivanov stood and pushed a button on a controller he was holding. A large screen came down on the far wall. He pushed another button, and within thirty or so seconds, a large image appeared on the screen. Putin stood and walked closer to the screen. The three men watched as two women dressed as French maids performed fellatio on a man lying on a bed.

Putin burst out laughing as he watched what unfolded before him on the screen. "By God, that is the president's chief of staff on that bed, isn't it?"

Anton Laino, the unofficial head of the Bratva or Russian Mafia, looked at Putin. "Indeed, it is, Mr. President. That is Frank Stillhouse, who seems to be enjoying himself immensely at the moment. That is happening at this very moment at the compound we built in southwestern rural Virginia.

"Stillhouse is the very first of senior American politicians who will have the pleasure of visiting with and enjoying our young ladies from Saint Petersburg."

Putin continued to laugh as he turned and looked at Laino. "That is brilliant, my friend. This is exactly what I wanted from this operation. While the Americans are focused on our meddling in their elections, they will never see this coming. So, Sergei, who will be next to fall into our sexual spiderweb?"

Ivanov smiled a deep and all-knowing smile. "None other than Ale Schumer, the Senate minority leader, is scheduled to be the next visitor to our sexual Shangri-La."

Putin grinned from ear to ear. "That is perfect, my friend. Our goal was to ensnare both Republican and Democratic leaders who will be useful puppets for us in the future." He walked over to the side cabinet near his desk. He reached in and took out a bottle of his favorite vodka. He filled three glasses and handed each a glass. He held up his glass and spoke, "Well done, my friends, and I do look forward to the next performance *as I so enjoy fucking American political idiots!*"

THE TRIP FROM QUINN'S HOUSE TO DR. JOHN'S OFFICE was but a ten-minute ride.

Dr. John had left a significant practice he was in charge of in a major metropolitan area in North Carolina to set up shop in rural southwest Virginia. He found himself in need of a change in scenery, as he tired of the business aspect of running a large medical practice. He quickly decided upon tiny Fancy Gap, Virginia, when he visited for the first time. The beautiful mountain vistas as well as the peaceful and serene way of life in this tiny mountain community suited him well.

His practice quickly swelled as the locals realized that such a seasoned and talented medical professional was now in their neck of the woods. They also benefited from his willingness to perform house calls for those who couldn't visit his office.

The flat rate of only forty dollars a visit was much-needed relief for those who were stuck beneath the poverty line. His presence was a godsend to many who never had access to quality and personal medical services.

Quinn parked his Ram in front of the office. Louisa jumped out and held Quinn's hand as they walked through the office door.

Nora, Dr. John's wife, who managed the office, smiled as Quinn and Louisa walked in. "Look who just walked in. We haven't seen you two in a spell. How long has it been? I bet it's been over a year since either of you two have been here.

"Now, Louisa, I understand you have been away for a while, but I heard you were back home. That news sure did make us happy!"

Louisa blushed as she walked over and hugged Nora. She smiled and looked at her. "I'm back and back for good. My life twisted and turned, and I turned when I should have twisted."

Just as she spoke, Dr. John came out of the examining room to the front office. "I heard that, Louisa. I'm here to tell you that we all have sometimes taken the wrong turn along this road of life. And only the bravest find a way to get back to the right place.

"Pray tell, what brings you two to see us today?"

Louisa turned and looked at Quinn. "Superman here is a little concerned about his stamina. Seems he can't keep up with me anymore on our bike rides. And it took a whole lot of convincing to get him here today."

Quinn rolled his eyes. "She is so dramatic. Listen, Doc, I'll admit that the ole get-up-and-go ain't what it used to be. But after all, I am a newly minted seventy-year-old. Shouldn't that have something to do with it, Doc?"

Dr. John stood and headed to the examining room. "Let's check you out from top to bottom and see what we have here."

Quinn followed him into the next room.

"Tell him the truth, McSpain," Louisa offered as he left.

Nora looked at Louisa after the door to the examining room closed. She smiled, reached out, and took Louisa's hands in hers. "So good to have you back where you belong, girl! I know he was heartbroken when you left."

"Nora, I had to go through hell before by the grace of God I found my way back to where my heart and soul belongs. A sage woman in New Mexico helped me see the light and gave me the courage to find my way back.

"That man in the next room welcomed me back with open arms and put all that happened behind him. I must be the luckiest woman on earth.

"But I am a bit concerned with his health. You understand that Quinn McSpain will be the last person on earth to complain about some ailment that is affecting his way of life. I'm so pleased he is with your husband in that room."

Dr. John put his stethoscope away after he listened to every part of Quinn's chest. He then examined his eyes as well as his ears. "So, at this point, I don't hear or see anything unusual. Your heart is beating well, and your lungs are clear. What sort of symptoms are you experiencing?"

Quinn shrugged. "Doc, besides being more tired than I should be after intense exercise, my feet have been real itchy from time to time. I'm talking about not a little itchy but intense want-to-scratch-my skin-off itchy."

Dr. John nodded. "Anything else?"

Quinn thought for a second. "Well, there is, come to think of it. From time to time, I see little black blotches in the corner of my eye. Not both eyes, mind you, but sometimes my right eye and, at times, my left. I'll rub my eyes, and usually in a few minutes, they disappear. Kinda strange, right?"

Dr. John took a few notes, then looked at Quinn as he put his pen down. "I think the next thing we do is a blood test. There is definitely something happening that a blood test might give us some insight into."

He stood and went to the medical cabinet to his right. Quinn flinched a bit when he realized that the good doctor was going to find a vein and take a blood sample.

Dr. John smiled as he swabbed the area where he was going to set the needle into Quinn's vein. "Nice veins you have there, Quinn. Relax 'cause this won't hurt."

Quinn watched the tube fill with his blood and held his finger on the gauze pad that Dr. John put on this arm. After the gauze was taped on, the doctor filled out the documentation paperwork to accompany the blood to the laboratory.

"Okay, we're through here, at least for now. I will get the results back in a couple of days, and with that, we will know more."

Quinn stood and looked at him. "Any preliminary thoughts as to what might be ailing me?"

Dr. John looked at him and smiled. "What I think now doesn't mean a thing, Quinn. I think your blood work should provide the clues I need to get to the bottom of this."

Quinn followed him out of the examining room.

Dr. John looked at Nora and Louisa. "I have good news . . . *he's not pregnant!*"

CHAPTER 13

LEVI SPREAD THE TOPOGRAPHY MAG ON THE CONFERENCE room desk. He set it beside the pages he had printed from Google Maps. He took a red pencil and circled the entire area around the Christian compound in Pipers Gap. He studied the maps and didn't hear the sheriff walk in. He turned as the sheriff came to his side.

"Levi, what have we got here?"

"Leroy, I had no idea how freaking big this whole operation is in Pipers Gap. They own some two hundred acres of land. Follow my finger as I follow the fence line around the property.

"Now look here, 'cause right under my finger is the guard house at the main entrance. And the main entrance seems to be the only entrance to that property. And look at all those buildings."

Leroy took a closer look at the maps. "How long has that place been open, Levi?"

"Heck, I don't know, Sheriff. I never paid that much attention to it when it was being built, as it was a church kinda place, and you know I don't cotton to any of that religious stuff, boss."

Leroy laughed at the comment. "Well, Levi, I'm going to suggest that you continue to dig around to see what you can come up with."

Levi shook his head in the affirmative as he folded the maps and looked at the sheriff. "I'm heading out that way right now to get a firsthand look at the place. I bet I can sweet-talk my way into that place."

The sheriff just shook his head as Levi walked out of the conference room and back to his desk. He put the maps back into his desk drawer and sat in his chair. He reached around to the other side of his desk and found his hiking boots. After he pulled them on and laced them up, he reached into the lower drawer of his desk and took out his binoculars and Nikon camera with the telephoto lens. He threw them in his backpack and headed for the parking lot door.

The sheriff's secretary watched him as he walked by. "Levi is off to hike the Appalachian Trail or off to the New River Trail to watch butterflies?"

Levi smiled. "Oh, hush, girl. I've been hired by National Geographic to take pictures."

He threw his gear into his pickup truck and headed down Highway 52 south heading to the Blue Ridge Parkway. He was pleased that he still had plenty of daylight left for what he needed to do. He was also pleased that he had his new Phantom drone he had bought at the Walmart in Galax.

This was just the operation where his drone might come in handy. Before he knew it, he passed over Pipers Gap Road on the parkway. He slowed and took the right off the parkway that would take him to Pipers Gap Road.

As he stopped at the stop sign, his cell phone rang. He looked down and saw Felicity's name on the screen. She was his longtime girlfriend whom he lived with. She moved in with him shortly after his last bout of unfaithfulness some time ago when he'd found himself involved with Libby Thomas.

He took a moment to decide if he should answer. He finally pushed the green answer button. "Hey, baby, what's your sweet little tush up to this afternoon?"

"Well, Levi Blackburn, I just got home from work, and I'm ready to get in that hot tub with lil ole you. So, when are you gonna be home? Won't be late, will you? I need my hunk of burning love home soon 'cause I'm . . . you know . . . I'm ready."

Levi smirked before he replied. "Felicity, I can feel your heat right through this dang phone, baby. But listen, you gonna have to put your little ole self on simmer for a bit 'cause I got some more work to do today."

There was a pause on the other end. "Levi, I hope you ain't bullshitting me right now! Where in the heck are ya?"

"Sweet thing, I just turned on Pipers Gap Road."

He waited a second before she replied, "What in Jesus's name are you doing in that sorry ass part of the county? You better not be visiting some new hottie you're trying to turn a trick for, your detective ass!"

"Felicity, hush! This is proper police business. There is some shit going down at this new religious compound they built off in the woods off of Pipers Gap Road. The sheriff sent me out to find out what in tarnation is going on out here."

Felicity didn't respond immediately. "You know, I read about that place when they built it in the *Galax Gazette* newspaper. I thought that was some weird shit when I read it back then. I wonder what kind of religious folks they are? They sure nuff can't be any new Mennonites moving into the area. Those Mennonites just don't have that kind of money. Couldn't they be Mormons? Those idiots like to build big temples. I remember when I saw the one they built in Winston-Salem."

Levi hated to interrupt her. "Darlin', I don't believe the Mormons have a place in Winston-Salem. But I do believe the Assembly of God have a pretty big place down there."

"Levi, how long you think you're gonna be tied up there? Will you be home for dinner? I got nice T-bone steaks I can cook up for us. And some nice strawberry shortcake for dessert."

"Dang girl that is making me hungry. Listen, I promise to be home in no more than two hours. I can't imagine it will take longer than that. Remember to put that hot body of yours on simmer 'til I get home!"

Levi waited for a response until she hung up. He set his phone down, but before he could take his hand off it, he saw that a text message had come through. What he saw was a naked Felicity licking her lips and smiling seductively.

Levi laughed and felt a surge in his manhood as he slowed to turn onto the road that led to the compound. He slowed his truck to a crawl, as he knew he was getting closer to the gate.

He stopped at the exact place he knew he needed to pull off the road and hide his truck. He turned to see the dirt road he was backing into. It didn't take long for him to be in the exact spot to hide the truck.

Once he turned the engine off, he stepped out on the dirt road. He paused for a moment and stood still. He didn't hear a thing. In a moment, he turned and opened the back door of his truck.

The drone case was set on the floor behind his backpack. He carefully removed the case and set it on top of the tonneau cover over the bed of the truck. The top came off as he unlatched the clips that held it on.

He closely looked over all the parts that were laid out in front of him in the case. Once he was satisfied that all the parts he needed were there, he latched the case closed.

The next thing he checked was his backpack. While his nine-millimeter pistol was on his hip, he also decided to bring a long-barrel forty-four magnum pistol in case he needed superior firepower.

Within five minutes, he was headed up the hill on the far side of the compound. His research indicated that a good vantage point was located several hundred feet above the compound on a ridge that was protected with low-hanging fir trees; he estimated this was the best place to launch his drone on its journey to surveil the property.

The hike up the ridge was more challenging than he expected. He had to struggle at several points to keep the drone case securely in his grasp. His hiking boots dug into the side of the steep embankment as he pulled himself up with his free hand.

Sweat droplets now poured off this forehead as he reached the top of the ridge. In a final motion, he swung the case in front of the spot where he planned to sit. It took a moment for Levi to catch his breath.

Once his breathing returned to normal, he pulled his legs around so he could comfortably see the landscape well below the ridge. He removed his binoculars from the backpack and scanned the landscape below him from east to west.

What impressed him the most was the sheer size of the compound. While his binoculars provided a glimpse of what was below him, Levi knew the drone was needed to get a bird's-eye view of exactly what was below him.

Once the drone was out of the case and on the ground in front of him, he switched the controller on. The unit came to life, and the screen lit up on the control panel.

With a flick of his finger, Levi instructed the drone to hover a few feet off the ground. Levi had become quite adept at using the drone on several past drug investigations. He also used it to spy on a neighbor who was cheating on his wife.

As the unit lifted off, he decided to direct it to the main entrance. Within two minutes, he had it hovering high above the entry road to the compound.

Just as he was about to direct it closer to the compound, his eye caught some movement coming down the access road. He dropped the drone down to get a better look. Once the drone hovered, he zoomed in to identify the vehicle that was approaching the compound.

He blinked as he looked closer at the screen before him. He stiffened and uttered, "*Holy shit!*"

ELENA SLOWLY OPENED THE DOOR WHERE FRANK Stillhouse was sprawled out on the bed. She knew he had been sleeping for at least six hours. His visit was about to expire in the next two hours.

During the past twenty-two hours, he had been serviced by all seven of the young ladies whose mission was to please him. Elena had watched the tapes of his sexual escapades and knew he had to be exhausted.

She took a long feather boa and gently massaged his body with it. It took long for him to start to stir. He slowly opened his eyes to see Elena setting his clothes out on the table near the bed he was lying on.

"How long have I been sleeping?" he asked and yawned.

Elena smiled. "About six hours, I would guess. But it is time to dress and get back to the helicopter that will take you home. I know Yuri wishes to visit with you before you leave."

Frank sat up and looked at Elena, who was nude. "Suppose I don't want to go home?" he offered as he stood from the bed.

Elena smiled, approached him, and took his hands. "But you must go home, my friend, as then you may return to see us some time in the future. I do hope that you enjoyed yourself?"

He laughed as he began to dress. "Oh, young lady, this past twenty-four hours has been a dream to me.

All my fantasies have been played out and then some. I could not have even imagined such an erotic experience with seven of the most beautiful women on the planet!"

Elena helped him finish dressing and took his hand as she led him out the door. As they approached the reception area, the door opened and Yuri appeared. Elena leaned over, kissed Frank, and whispered, "I certainly hope to see you again!" With that, she left through another door.

Yuri led Frank to the main reception area. He motioned for him to sit in one of the two chairs. "Frank, the helicopter is ready when you are. Can I get you a Bloody Mary?"

Frank smiled. "Perfect!"

Yuri mixed two drinks and handed one to Frank. He held his glass high. "Cheers, my friend. I hope your visit exceeded your expectations."

Frank savored the first sip. "Nothing—and I mean nothing—could have been better that the past twenty-three or so hours I've been here. This was heaven on earth and exactly what I needed at this time in life. You and your young women provided moments of exotic pleasure that were never less than exquisite!"

Yuri smiled and sipped his drink. "Frank, that is why we are here, my friend. We offer what doesn't exist anywhere else on this planet. Having said that, I must ask your highest level of discretion in regard to your experience.

"While others of similar station in life as yourself are scheduled to visit, this is the sort of opportunity that can be known to but a select few. I'm sure you understand."

Frank finished his drink and stood. "Yuri, you have nothing to worry about as far as I'm concerned. Your secret is safe with me. After all, I can only hope to return in the not-too-distant future."

Yuri smiled as he led Frank to the helicopter pad. The pilot held the door open, and Frank shook Yuri's hand and climbed aboard. He smiled as the pilot closed the door.

Frank felt a hand on his shoulder; the young lady who had been with him on the flight to the compound was again present. She took the hood and gently placed it over his head. She started to massage his back as the helicopter took off.

Frank laughed out loud as he thought, *It can't get any better than this!*

LOUISA LOOKED AT QUINN AS THEY LEFT THE DOCTOR'S office and headed back to his house. She looked at the piece of gauze on his arm, which covered the spot where his blood was taken. Her thoughts began to float through the possibilities of what malaise was somewhere in the body of the man she so loved.

She was watching the road ahead and didn't notice the smile on Quinn's face as he looked at her. "So, my dearest Louisa, I just can't imagine what your inquisitive, investigative mind is churning through right now."

Louisa waited a moment before she replied, "Big man, I can only imagine what has turned you into such a crybaby. You will do anything to wimp out on anything that requires you to keep up with me."

Quinn smiled as he drove and was about to reply when his phone rang. The sheriff's name flashed upon the screen. He pushed the hands-free button. "If it isn't the esteemed sheriff of Carroll County on the line. I'm surprised you even remember who we are."

"This is Quinn McSpain I'm talking with, isn't it? I think I must have misdialed."

Quinn and Louisa burst into laughter and Louisa offered, "Why, Sheriff, you indeed have reached that nefarious McSpain fellow. And today he has been pressed into duty as my personal driver."

The sheriff roared, "Finally an occupation that suits his skills. Exactly where are you two?"

"We have just left Dr. John's office, and we are headed home. Pray tell, do I dare ask why you are calling?"

"Oh, you can ask, but let's see. Since I'm at home and haven't gone to the office yet, you can make a few turns and join Laneisha and me for a cup of coffee at the farm. Can you make that work?"

Louisa nodded to Quinn. "Leroy, I believe we might just like to enjoy some of Laneisha' s fine coffee right now. See you in ten minutes."

Quinn ended the call and took the next left turn. "What do you think that is all about?" he asked.

Louisa shook her head. "I haven't a clue. But if memory serves me right, I think our good sheriff wants to share something with us."

Quinn shook his head. "God . . . *I can only imagine.*"

———

SUE ANN KOLLMAN SLOWED DOWN AS SHE APPROACHED the main gate at the compound. She stopped in front of the gate and looked at the gate house as the main door opened. A well-dressed young man came out to greet her. She pressed the button, and her driver's side window came down.

The man smiled. "Can I help you, miss?"

Lee Ann choked a bit. "I have an appointment with Yuri."

The young man smiled still. "And your name please?"

She paused for a moment before replying, "Sue Ann Kollman."

He turned and went back into the gate house. Within a few moments, the massive bronze gate with two crosses perfectly centered in the middle started to open. The young man returned to her car and smiled. "Ms. Kollman, Yuri is expecting you. Please follow the signs to the reception area, and someone will greet you there."

Sue Ann smiled as she closed her window and slowly drove through the gates. She was immediately taken with the beautiful trees and flowers that lined the long, winding road. She could see that no expense had been spared when it came to the landscaping.

The sign ahead of her directed her to a small parking lot in front of the reception area. She looked around and admired the grounds before she got out of her car. As she did, the main door of the reception area opened, and a tall, well-dressed man walked toward her car.

He smiled and extended his hand as he approached her. "Welcome, Ms. Kollman. So pleased that you decided to visit us today. My name is Yuri."

Sue Ann blushed, and they shook hands. "Well, I guess I'm happy to be here as well. This is such a beautiful place. Your grounds are perfect."

"Sue Ann, we take pride in what we do and what we have put in place here. But please follow me so I can show you the rest of our buildings."

She walked beside him into the reception area. She was impressed with the furniture and beautiful artwork hanging on the walls. While she was not an expert on art, she was impressed by what she saw.

Within a few minutes, they entered another area where he opened the door to what appeared to be an office. Yuri motioned for Sue Ann to sit on the couch on the near side of his desk. He sat near her on the couch, crossed his legs, and looked at her with a smile on his face.

She looked around his office and offered, "This is the most beautiful office I have ever seen."

"Why, you haven't seen the best part." With that, he pushed a button on the remote by his side on the couch. The wall panels behind his desk began to slide open. As they did, Sue Ann was taken by what appeared before her.

She could now see the mountain ridges off in the distance. The sun was beginning to set, and since his office enjoyed a perfect southern exposure, she could see the sun beginning to set off in the distant western sky.

"My God, that is beautiful. This is all truly amazing."

He smiled and looked at her. "Sue Ann, we have spared no expense on this operation. I'm certain that Tommie Cruz provided some detail as to who we are. Your friend was a valuable asset to us, and we are sorry that he is gone forever.

"You are in a position to gain from not only what you have seen but what you can do for us in the future. We are willing to provide you with ample compensation for your services. But first, let us review the matter at hand.

"I understand that one of our young ladies passed you a note while in the supermarket. Do you have the note with you?"

Sue Ann reached into her bag, took out a piece of folded paper and handed it to Yuri. He slowly unfolded it and read it. He then set it beside him on the couch. "Now comes the important part. You must look at our young ladies and tell me who handed the note to you." Having said that, he punched another button on the remote, and another panel opened on the opposite wall.

A massive eighty-two-inch 4 Ultra HD screen came to life. She squinted for a moment as her eyes adjusted.

Yuri smiled. "What you see are seven young women who are doing a daily aerobics routine. It is vital that all of the women on our staff stay in top physical shape."

Sue Ann could not keep her eyes off of the seven women going through their routines on the screen before her. She was certain she had never seen any women as beautiful as those she was looking at. She was even more taken by the fact that all they were wearing was their gym shoes. She stood and walked closer to the screen to admire the perfection of all seven she was looking at.

"Sue Ann, they are perfect, aren't they? They work hard at what they do, and they deliver the intended results for us. Now take a close look and tell me which one handed you the note."

It didn't take long for her to zero in on Elena. She was taken with her perfect body and the ease with which she performed the aerobic routines. In a moment, she turned and pointed at Elena. "She is the one."

Without showing it, Yuri cringed, as he so favored Elena over the others.

Sue Ann looked at him. "Are you surprised?" she asked.

Yuri didn't look at her as he answered, "No, nothing surprises me. While I'm disappointed, I'm not surprised. This young lady is Elena. She is one of the smarter of our girls. That is probably why she took a risk.

"But, Sue Ann, that is a challenge we are equipped to deal with. Your help has been extremely valuable." Having said that, he stood and walked over to his desk. He opened a bottom drawer, removed a small satchel, and walked back to the couch.

He sat as he set the satchel next to Sue Ann. "Inside this bag is $100,000. What you did means a lot to us, and there is more to come if you can be of assistance from time to time.

"Tommie told me some time ago that you are smart with your money. I have no qualms that you will not squander this money away. That is not all that Tommie told me. He passed along that you like to be with women as well as you do with men."

Sue Ann straightened up a bit on the couch.

Yuri held his hand up. "Sue Ann, I'm not here to judge you. On the contrary—I'm here to help you. Please do look at the girls again and tell me if any arouse you in any way."

Sue Ann slowly stood and walked toward the screen. She took her time before she replied. She felt the lust stir from within. She looked at Yuri and pointed at the redhead on the far side of the screen.

Yuri smiled as he stood and walked over to Sue Ann. He took her hand. "That is Inga, and within a few moments . . . *she will be yours!*"

FRANK STILLHOUSE SAT AT HIS KITCHEN TABLE AND FINished his last cup of coffee as he quickly perused *The New York Times* as well as *The Washington Post*, which were spread out on the table in front of him. He looked at his watch and smiled as he saw it was seven thirty and he was right on time.

He was enjoying this time alone, as his wife, Phyllis, had not yet returned from her skiing trip with her girlfriends. He knew her dirty little secret that her lover was to be with her on the skiing holiday. None of that mattered to him, as he understood that his was a marriage of convenience. She had inherited a large sum of money from her parents' estate, which allowed them to live rather well.

He looked toward his driveway to see that his driver and bodyguard were right on time. He greeted his housekeeper when they crossed paths as he left. Within five minutes, he was sitting in the back seat of the car, checking on his appointments for the day.

One of the appointments caught his eye. He hadn't recalled a scheduled meeting with the Russian Ambassador Sergey Kisiyak. He quickly texted a message to his secretary. She replied immediately and suggested that Kisiyak had called late on the previous day to schedule a meeting.

After his driver parked, Stillhouse walked through the White House corridors, heading past the Oval Office to his corner office.

He greeted his secretary as he stopped to pick up messages at her desk. "Well, Helen, are there any other surprises awaiting me this morning?"

Helen had worked for Stillhouse in the private sector and was a key cog in the wheel that kept his office operational. She smiled and looked toward the Oval Office. "Our commander in chief is on the war path. Seems he has his panties in a knot over a piece in *The New York Times* this morning."

Frank read through the slips she handed him. "I'm not surprised. I read the article this morning, and it is bullshit. Those bastards at the *Times* have it out for us. Has he been looking for me?"

Helen giggled. "No, not yet. But we know that won't last, don't we."

Frank smiled as he went into his office and closed the door. He sat at his desk and knew his first conference call was in five minutes. Once he was through his briefing notes on the call, he punched in a few numbers on his phone and was connected.

For the next two hours, he went from call to call before he looked up to see Helen come in his office and hand him a note. He looked at his office clock and realized Kislyak was right on time.

He covered the mouthpiece on his phone and looked at Helen. "Show him in in five minutes."

She nodded as she left the office.

Frank hung up after the call ended and still wondered exactly what the Russian ambassador was up to. Just as he was about to stand, Helen knocked on the door.

"Come in, come in, Mr. Ambassador," he offered as he stood to greet the tall Russian. He offered him a seat in front of his desk, and Frank decided to be informal and sit in the chair across from him.

"Frank, I am so pleased that you could see me this morning," the Russian said.

"Why, Sergey, I knew this must be important, as you normally call for routine matters. So, while I have no idea what you are here for, I'm certain it must be important. Would you like some coffee or tea perhaps?"

"No, that is not necessary. Let me get to the heart of the matter. There are two matters at hand. The first is that you must convince the president to ease the sanctions against Russia. They are hurting us economically and need to end.

"The second is that the United States must back off your efforts in Syria. We are fully engaged in our own assistance in the area and cannot afford a confrontation with your country. Now I know what you are thinking. And no, I have not lost my mind. I must suggest you use the vast influential powers your have with the president to convince him to take these steps."

Frank leaned back and rubbed his forehead. "To begin, Sergey, I'm shocked that you are even here asking for these ridiculous actions to be taken on the president's part. This has really caught me off guard.

"Let me make my opinions perfectly clear to you. First of all, I drew up the sanctions in the first place. The man down the hall would think I was a fucking idiot if I walked in there with that request.

"As far as our operations in Syria go, I plan to go in and see the president today and suggest that we up the ante as far as our operations go there. So, my friend I believe you have wasted some of your valuable time by coming here to suggest any of this."

Sergey didn't respond for a moment. "Frank, I do believe you will be in a position to support these requests."

After saying that, he reached into his breast pocket and took out his phone. "As a matter of fact, I'm quite certain that you will be an avid supporter of what we are asking for." He pushed few buttons on his phone and turned the screen to Frank for him to see.

He slowly handed the phone to Frank, who now was watching Elena and Natalia service him on the circular bed. He dropped the phone in front of him.

Sergey picked it up, stood, and handed a flash drive to Frank. "I will leave now, but you must now do what needs to be done for us." He turned and walked out of Frank's office.

Frank looked down to the floor in stunned disbelief. He stood and slowly walked to his chair behind his desk. He slumped into it and never saw Helen come in the office.

"Are you okay, Frank?" she asked.

He waved her away. "Cancel my calls for the next hour."

She nodded and left the office.

He slumped in his chair and slipped the flash drive into his personal laptop. The images started with his getting into the helicopter. He watched for at least five minutes, then pulled the drive out as he realized they had captured all of it.

He softly pounded his desk with his left hand as he opened the bottom right drawer of his desk. He was frozen in his seat as he looked at his thirty-eight-caliber pistol in the bottom of the drawer. *His head dropped as his hand reached. . . .*

CHAPTER 14

QUINN ADMIRED THE ROLLING HILLS LEADING UP THE sheriff's farmhouse. Along with his wife, Laneisha, they farmed over one hundred acres of land. His farm implements as well as his tractors were parked by his massive barn.

Laneisha waved at them as Quinn pulled up to the house. Louisa was first to get out of the truck. She had not seen Laneisha since her return to Fancy Gap. They met at the first step to the porch and embraced.

"God, I'm so happy you are back with us, Louisa."

Tears started to flow from both women's eyes as they held hands and walked up the stairs. Quinn could feel the emotion between them, and he kept his place a few feet back. Leroy came through the screen door holding a tray full of coffee cups and a large pot of coffee.

Quinn looked at him. "Laneisha, I sure do hope you were the one who brewed that pot of coffee. That husband of yours has a few skills, but brewing coffee sure isn't one of his best."

The sheriff laughed. "Quinn McSpain, you sure nuff will never be taken for one with any culinary skills whatsoever. And yes, I brewed this pot."

All four of them laughed as Leroy filled each of their cups.

Laneisha sat next to Louisa and held her hand. Louisa began to tear up and was about to say something when Laneisha held her hand up. "Not a word, girlfriend. Not one peep, do you hear? What has happened is in the past. We all live among saints and sinners, and we all take our turns in those categories. All that is important, and I mean all that is important is that you are back and with the man you love."

They stood and hugged each other for a long time. Quinn sipped his coffee and waited until they both sat. "Laneisha, I really do give you credit. Most women would have packed their bags a long time ago if their main man couldn't do a better job with coffee than Leroy does. This stuff is mud!"

The four burst out laughing before Leroy held up his hands. "Okay, enough of this. I really do need to run something by you two."

Quinn looked at Louisa. "See, I told you so. He is up to his ears in something, and he needs our help. Tell me that ain't so, Leroy?"

"Okay, Mr. Smarty-Pants, there is a little something you both need to digest for me. A week or so ago, a couple was killed and burned in their little cabin in a very remote section of Pipers Gap. This husband and wife were two lost souls living off the land in Carroll County.

"So, we just couldn't figure out why anyone would want to kill those two. Well, my favorite detective—yes, none other than Levi—discovered that they had set up a wildlife camera at the beginning of the access road to their cabin. He dug deeper into this all and discovered that the last vehicle to enter and leave the property was an SUV with a plate registered to the Christian group that built the massive compound in Pipers Gap.

"So, Levi is over in the area using our drone to see whatever he can in and around the property. But all of this has raised question marks in my mind as to what is going on over there."

Louisa perked up and looked at the sheriff. "I must have missed all of this. Exactly who built a religious conference center in Pipers Gap?"

Leroy scratched his head. "That is a good question. I researched all of the documents they submitted to the county when they built the place. The best I can determine is that this center was funded by several small Christian groups—from California, of all places.

"I talked with our county manager, who was invited to tour the facility when it was completed, and he was very impressed with the management team he met when he went there."

Quinn took another sip of coffee before he spoke. "I did read something about this conference center in an article in the *Galax Gazette*. I guess if memory serves me right, I thought it was somewhat weird that any group would build such a substantial facility in Pipers Gap of all places.

"If they are somehow connected to the horrific deaths of two poor innocent souls, I start to wonder what could have possibly been the motive for such a killing?

"Those two didn't have two quarters to rub together, so I think we can rule out drugs."

Before he could continue, Louisa jumped in. "No, those two saw something they shouldn't have seen. And the killers wanted to silence them forever. But why? What did they see?"

The sheriff loved that Quinn and Louisa were getting engaged in the matter. Before he could say another word, his cell phone rang. Levi's name flashed up on the screen. Leroy hit the answer button. "What's up, Levi? I'm sitting on my porch, and I just updated Quinn and Louisa on the whole mystery out there in Pipers

Gap." He stopped to listen to what Levi had to say and then hung up.

"Okay, Levi just got back from Pipers Gap and is in the office. He has some footage from the drone camera he wants us to see. So, finish your coffee and let's head to my office."

Quinn and Louisa looked at each other and smiled.

Leroy looked at them both. "Okay, you two. I promise to try and not get you killed. I just need your brains and deductive reasoning to help us find out what is going on out there!"

Louisa took Quinn's hand and headed to his truck. Once they were inside and buckled in, Louisa looked at Quinn. "I just knew he had something in store for us. . . . *I just knew it!*"

YURI LED SUE ANN THROUGH SEVERAL CORRIDORS THAT connected different buildings. He stopped before one that was adorned with an aquatic theme. He opened it and led Sue Ann in. She looked around and was taken back by a system of small pools that fed into one another.

He looked at her and smiled. "Enjoy yourself," he whispered as he left the room.

Sue Ann looked up and saw the redheaded woman she had selected standing at the top of the circular stairway that flowed down next to each pool. She was wearing a long, pink, silk robe that flowed open as she descended the stairs.

She smiled as she slowly descended the last set of stairs that ended where Sue Ann was standing. Sue Ann couldn't take her eyes away from this statuesque woman coming toward her.

While Sue Ann was almost six feet tall, this redheaded woman was a bit taller. Sue Ann licked her dry lips as the woman stopped no more than twelve inches from her.

"Sue Ann, my name is Inga, and I am so pleased that you have joined me today. I look forward to our time together."

Before Sue Ann could reply, Inga brought her hands up to Sue Ann's cheeks, and their lips met. Sue Ann felt a jolt of lust flow through every inch of her body. She trembled as Inga slowly brought her hands down to Sue Ann's blouse and stated to unbutton the top button.

Sue Ann trembled even more as Inga slowly un-hooked her bra and dropped it to the floor. While Sue Ann was proud of her own firm breasts, she marveled at the creamy white firmness of Inga's breasts.

Inga smiled as she took Sue Ann's left hand and began using it to massage her breast. Soon, Sue Ann raised her left hand and started to accommodate the other.

Inga closed her eyes and began to breathe deeply as she enjoyed Sue Ann's massage. Her nipples hardened between Sue Ann's fingers. The effect was not lost on Sue Ann as she began to feel the moisture between her legs.

Inga's hands loosened the top of Sue Ann's slacks. Within a moment, she slowly slid them down to Sue Ann's ankles. She dropped to one knee to remove the slacks and Sue Ann's shoes.

All that remained was Sue Ann's panties. Inga dropped to both knees and began to lick Sue Ann's belly button. From there, she bit the top of her panties and slowly pulled them down to her ankles.

Inga stood and smiled as she passionately kissed Sue Ann. She then took her hand and led her to the edge of the bottom pool. They sat side-by-side on the smooth edge of the bottom pool. The warm water from the pool above slowly caressed their shoulders.

Sue Ann spread her legs as Inga's hand gently found its way. Inga smiled as she felt Sue Ann's hand exploring between her legs. Both women moaned as they massaged each other into orgasmic states.

Inga slowly slipped down in front of Sue Ann's open legs. She bent back and started to kiss Sue Ann's feet. Sue Ann moaned deeply as Inga worked her way passed Sue Ann's knees to her open legs.

Sue Ann lay back in ecstasy as the water cascaded all over her breasts. Her mind swirled as Inga's tongue began to slowly caress her clitoris. The circular motions created more stimulation than she had ever experienced.

Her hips started to pound the bottom of the pool as Inga's finger explored her anal cavity and her tongue worked its own magic. Sue Ann convulsed into orgasm after orgasm as her juices flowed freely all over Inga's face.

Sue Ann yelled with pleasure, "Don't stop . . . don't ever stop!"

Yuri smiled as he watched on the large screen in his office. *"Not to worry. We won't. . . . "*

———

THE PRESIDENT WALKED OUT OF HIS OFFICE AND HEADED down the hall. He walked into Frank's office and stopped at Helen's desk. "Is he in?"

Helen blushed. "Why, yes, Mr. President, he is."

With that, the president opened the door and walked in. He stopped dead in his tracks. Frank Stillhouse was standing in front of his window. He was holding his revolver in his right hand and a bottle of whiskey in his left hand.

The president slowly walked toward him. "So, do you plan to drink by yourself, or will you share some with me?"

Frank turned and looked at him. "Mr. President, I need to be alone. You don't need to see this."

"You're right—I don't need to see this, and I don't plan to. A man shouldn't drink alone or die alone. So, we just have to determine what happens next. I don't have a clue as what might have happened that has the man who I have the upmost respect and trust for in such a precarious moment. But rest assured, Frank, there is nothing you could have possibly done that you should end a great life over. So, set your pistol down, and sit down with me while we have a drink."

Frank didn't move for the longest time until the president went to the cabinet, took out another glass, and sat down. Frank went to his desk and put his pistol down. He then slowly walked over and sat opposite the president.

There was an unnerving silence in the room for the longest time.

"Frank, are you going to squeeze that bottle to death, or do I get some?"

Frank hesitated for a moment before he handed the bottle to the president. He laughed as he poured some whiskey into his glass. "I must say, it has been many a year since I have sipped Wild Turkey 101 before ten o'clock in the morning."

The president leaned forward and held out his glass. "Cheers, my friend, because nothing could possibly be that bad."

With that, the president took a sip and set his glass down. Frank brought his glass to his lips but stopped short of taking a sip. He slowly set his glass back on the table. He brought both of his hands up to his cheeks and began to sob.

The president sat and watched him for a moment. "While I never expected to see you sob, I must admit I'm really anxious to hear what brought you to this precipice."

Frank wiped the tears from his cheeks and looked just past the president. "I'm so pissed off at myself. I fucked up royally, and now I'm under pressure to do something I just don't want to do. I just really fucked up."

The president took another sip. "Frank, you're a really bright guy who hardly ever drops the ball. Hell, I wish I could say that for myself. But the fact that you screwed up is intriguing. Please do share what has happened."

"Mr. President, I just don't know where to begin."

The president smiled and sat back as he took another sip. "At the beginning, Frank. At the beginning."

"I guess it started when I was talking to Dan Nelson. I know you've met Dan before—he has been a generous contributor to your campaigns as well as to the party. So, he talked with me and went on and on about a very special twenty-four hours he had spent at some retreat in Europe. It turns out, a brand-new one is hidden in a remote area of southwest Virginia. He suggested that the kind of sexual experience offered there might just be what I need to take a break from all of this.

"So, I eventually gave in and he made all the arrangements. Heck, he even paid the fee for the experience. I must admit that I was excited about the whole thing.

"Listen, I also know that Phyllis is having an affair with some young stud who shacked up with her in Colorado. Frankly, I'm happy for her. We are happy together in a brother-and-sister kind of relationship.

"All of that convinced me that an exciting twenty-four hours with some beautiful women might be just right for my libido. I met a private helicopter in Great Falls, and off I went. The excitement started right away. A young woman was with me on the flight. She was inarguably one of the most beautiful women I have ever seen. We were in the air no more than ten minutes when she performed the best blow job I have ever experienced."

The president took another sip of his drink and leaned forward. "And then what happened?"

"Well, she blindfolded me, so I didn't have a clue where we landed, but it didn't take that long to get there. I was met by a professional man named Yuri. At first, I thought he might be Russian, but he didn't have accent. His English was perfect.

"Then the party started. I was introduced to seven of the most beautiful women on this planet. All different-looking but impeccable in every way—and so very easy on the eyes. While they were all very young, I must say they knew what they were doing.

"In the twenty-four hours I was there, I was sucked and fucked in ways I could have never imagined. They knew how to bring me to the brink of excitement and back off ever so gently so I could continue along."

The president loosened his tie. "Frank, fill up my glass 'cause I need to hear more."

"I can do better than tell you. Let me get my computer, and you can see for yourself."

Frank went to desk and brought his personal laptop around to the table in front of the president. He tuned it on and inserted the flash drive. The very first image to come up was the young lady on the helicopter. They both sat back and watched what appeared to be some fifteen minutes of video footage.

Once it concluded, the president sat back and looked at Frank. "Now I have a reason to be upset. For crying out loud, why in hell didn't you take me! I'm with you on this one—those were the seven most beautiful women I have ever seen as well. Absolutely gorgeous! I must say, you handled yourself well under some very challenging conditions there, Frank. Pretty impressive!

"So, exactly when did you get the flash drive?"

"This morning. Sergey Kislyak dropped by and suggested I should try to influence you on lifting sanctions on Russia and backing off in Syria."

The president erupted in laughter. "Did those fucking idiots think they could blackmail us with this crap? I just don't believe it. Really lame of them."

The president stood and walked over to Frank's desk. He picked up his pistol and looked at Frank. "Two things, my friend. The first is put this thing away and lock it up. The second, get your friend Nelson in so we can have a friendly little chat with him. I want to find out exactly who his Russian friends are."

He started to walk out of the office and stopped. He went back to Frank's desk and picked up the flash drive. *"Let me hold on to this for a while."*

CHAPTER 15

THE SHERIFF ARRIVED BACK TO HIS OFFICE WITH QUINN and Louisa close behind. Once they settled into his office, Levi came by. "Okay, you three, let's look at my drone footage in the conference room."

Quinn and Louisa followed the sheriff into the conference room and sat next to Levi. Quinn could tell that Levi was agitated. He sat there shaking his head from side to side.

The sheriff looked at him. "Let's see what you got, Levi."

"Leroy, I'm warning you—this will piss you off. I just don't know what to think." Levi started the tape and explained where he had been and described the buildings in the compound. Some ten minutes into the tape, he stopped it. "This is what I'm all confounded about." He set the tape speed on slow motion. All watched as a truck came down the access road and approached the main gate. The truck stopped, and the driver rolled the window down to talk with the man who came out of the gate house.

The sheriff was the first to speak. "Is that Sue Ann Kollman, or am I seeing things here?"

"No, boss, your eyes aren't deceiving you. That is Sue Ann's truck, and she is driving it. And it didn't take long before the gate opened, and they let her in. Like they were expecting her or something," Levi blurted out.

Quinn looked at Louisa. "This is the same place where the suspects in the couple's killing are from? Is that right?"

Levi looked at him. "Spot on, Quinn McSpain. That is the two and two I put together. I wish I could have stayed longer, but I couldn't risk being detected by whoever lives there.

"I'm here to tell you I'm really surprised that they didn't see me because that place is protected with some pretty sophisticated security equipment. Trust me, no one gets close to that place without them knowing.

"My bet is that ole Rufus and Gearleen stumbled upon that place and probably got a wee bit too curious. And that is what cost them their lives."

The sheriff continued to look at the screen before him. "So, what in the world is Sue Ann doing there? Levi, did she know of your interest in that place?"

"No sirree bob, she didn't! I never discussed that with her at all," Levi offered.

Louisa looked at the sheriff. "I have talked to Sue Ann a few times in passing, and she always seemed like a young law enforcement professional. Have there been any problems with her in the past? What is her social life like?"

Levi stood. "We have never had a problem with her. Sue Ann is one of the best deputies we have. Hard worker and a team player. Now I'm not so sure about her social life. I heard some time back that she was seeing some fella over in Galax, but I never saw her with anyone.

"Come to think of it, my girlfriend, Felicity, did come to know her a little bit from some of the department social parties, and she got the impression that, after a few drinks, Sue Ann was coming on to her. But that could be Felicity's imagination 'cause she likes to think that both men and women are attracted to her."

The sheriff spoke, "Levi is right—Sue Ann is one of the best in my book. I'm shocked by all of this. We need to find out what she was doing there. We also need to deep dive into just who the residents of that compound are." The sheriff looked at Louisa. "After we find out a bit more about that group, I will question Sue Ann as to why she was there. Louisa, I would appreciate it if you could be here when I talk to her. I know she trusts and respects you."

Louisa looked at Quinn. "Leroy, I can do that. But in the meantime, I'm going to do a bit of digging with my friends in Washington to see what we can find out about this group."

Leroy smiled. "Thanks, Louisa, that is certainly appreciated. Okay, folks, let's get to it and see what unravels here."

Quinn and Louisa didn't talk until they settled into Quinn's truck. He looked at her. "It sure didn't take long for us to get invited into another Carroll County mystery. I thought we were finished with this sort of thing."

Louisa reached over and took his hand. *"McSpain, you love it and you know it!"*

———

PRESIDENT ROGERS LOOKED UP A NUMBER ON HIS PHONE and dialed. The phone rang several times before his call was answered.

"To what do I owe the honor of having the president call me?" Dan Nelson looked out the window of his estate along the Potomac River and allowed his mind to wander to why Craig Rogers was calling.

"Relax, Dan, I'm not calling for money. That will come when I'm in the reelection cycle. I know this is short notice, but can you see me at the White House this afternoon?"

Nelson opened his appointment book and saw he was free after two o'clock. "This is your lucky day, Mr. President. I can be there at two thirty; will that work?"

"Why, Dan, that is just right. See you at two thirty."

Nelson set his phone down and looked at the river below him. His mind drifted through the possible reasons the president wanted to see him. Nothing immediately jumped out as red flags.

President Rogers punched in a speed dial number on his cell phone. Not far from the White House at the Headquarters of the Federal Bureau of Investigation, the director, Sandy Winston, saw the president's name on his phone.

"Good morning, Mr. President," Winston offered.

"Good morning, Sandy. I know this is short notice, but can you be in my office at two thirty this afternoon?"

"Let me check. . . . I can adjust a thing or two to make that work. Is there anything I need to do to prepare?" he asked.

"No, Sandy, I will fill you in when you get here. Thanks!"

After the president hung up, Winston made a few calls to reset his schedule. He then poured himself another cup of coffee as he wondered what the president of the United Sates had in store for him.

The rest of the morning flew by, and suddenly Winston realized he needed to head to the White House.

He soon found himself on the way to the garage, where his driver was waiting for him.

In no time, they were darting through the mess they called traffic in the District of Columbia. Luckily, lunchtime traffic had subsided a bit, and they made it to the White House gate in no time.

Winston got out of his car and clipped on his White House badge. The Marine at the door opened it for him, and he found his way to the Oval Office waiting area. The receptionist greeted him and advised that the president was running a few minutes late.

As he checked his emails on his phone, he saw another man approaching the reception area. He wasn't exactly sure if he recognized the man until he got closer.

He had met Dan Nelson at a few White House social gatherings he'd attended. He knew the man's reputation as a billionaire investor who had made a fortune in tech stocks. He also knew that he'd never come across any intelligence that Nelson was involved in any criminal activity.

Nelson sat next to him. "This makes this summons to the Oval Office all the more interesting. I don't think I have done anything that should interest the director of the Federal Bureau of Investigation, but who knows."

Sandy Winston smiled. "Dan, I think if you had you might have met some of my staff beforehand."

Nelson laughed, but before he could respond, the president's secretary appeared. "Gentlemen, he is ready to see you."

Nelson led the way into the Oval Office. The president was on a call and motioned for them to be seated. He finished quickly and joined them after he set his phone down. "Get you anything to drink?" he asked.

"No, not me," Nelson replied.

"Just water for me, Mr. President," Winston answered.

The president went to his small refrigerator and removed two bottles of Evian water. He handed one to Winston as he sat down.

"I know you two can't imagine why you are both here at the same time. I'll admit it is kind of weird, but our lives are weird from time to time or, as some would think about me, all of the time."

Both Nelson and Winston chuckled at the comment.

"Gentlemen, this is all about Frank Stillhouse."

Nelson stiffened for a moment.

"Dan, I believe you know why I might be bringing this to your attention. You are just probably surprised that you're hearing it from me. To be truthful, I'm more surprised than the both of you.

"Sandy, let me give you the Reader's Digest condensed version of what's going on here because you don't have a clue. To begin, ole Dan here set Frank up with a terrific twenty-four-hour getaway in some bumfuck part of southwest Virginia. Unbeknownst to Frank, this little trip was nothing less than a fuck fest he enjoyed with at least seven women. Now you might be thinking, well, who really gives a shit if my chief of staff heads off to God knows only where to screw his brains out?

"Under normal circumstances, I couldn't have cared less. But, gentlemen, these are not normal circumstances.

"Guess who showed up this morning to pay ole Frank a visit? Well, you will never guess, so I'll tell you. None other than Sergey Kislyak, our esteemed Russian ambassador, came by this morning and suggested that Frank use his influence with me to change my position on economic sanctions against Russia and back out of my policy on Syria.

"I know you both are thinking, *Why in the world would he force Frank to make those suggestions to me?* Let me show you."

The president picked up a remote control from the table in front of him and pushed a button. A screen came out of the ceiling in front of them. He pushed another button, and the screen came alive with the video with Frank in the starring role.

The president didn't say a word until the video ended. He looked at them both and smiled. "Wow, Frank Stillhouse is one of the luckiest men on earth. Did you see those women? Good gracious, I'm still laden with envy.

"Dan, you must play a key role in all of this since you set this up for Frank and paid for it, didn't you?"

Nelson cleared his throat. "That is correct, Mr. President. I did indeed. Guilty as charged, at least for the trip part. I had no idea that the Russians would think they could use such a thing to blackmail him to influence you."

Winston began taking notes. "Dan, help us out here. How did you even know this place existed?"

Nelson looked at Winston. "This was all kind of sudden. A Russian business contact, Yuri Dobrow, reached out to me and asked if I knew of anyone who might enjoy the ultimate erotic twenty-four hours. I have heard of businessmen who have experienced such adventures in Europe.

"I know that Frank has been working his butt off as your chief of staff. My natural instinct was that was something I could do for my dear friend."

Winston stopped writing. "What do we know of this Yuri fellow, and where did the helicopter leave from?"

"Just as I told you, he is a respected businessman who, as far as I know, is above board. I just don't know him that well. And Frank got picked up in Great Falls."

The president stood. "Gentlemen, there you have it. Sandy, I need you to utilize your vast resources to find out who this Yuri is and exactly where this sexual Shangri-La is located. We need to take them out of business. Hell, for all we know, they just might have another politician lined up for the experience."

Winston stood and shook the president's hand. "We will get on this immediately and determine what needs to get done here. It shouldn't take us long."

Both men started to leave when the president chimed in, "And Dan—not a word to anyone on this."

Nelson paused. "Not a peep, Mr. President. I promise."

The door to the Oval Office closed, and the president sat back on the couch. He picked up the remote and clicked the video on again. *"I need to see those women again. . . . "*

——◆——

DR. JOHN READ THE LAB REPORTS FROM THE BLOOD work he had submitted from the day before. He stopped when he came to Quinn's blood work. His hematocrit number was way out of whack. The normal level was thirty-eight to forty-five. Quinn's number was sixty-nine, and that was of concern.

He understood that Quinn might have a significant risk of a sudden stroke due to a blood clot from his thick red blood cells. What he needed to find out was the cause of his heightened count.

He took out his phone and looked up a name and number. Dr. Jackson was an oncologist in Winston-Salem whom he had referred patients to in the past. She was loved by the folks he sent down to her. He knew she was the best choice for Quinn.

He put in her number and started to type in a text message. He hit the send button, and his message was on its way. No more than three minutes later, her reply found its way to his phone.

"Great to hear from you! I look forward to meeting Mr. McSpain. Have him call my office for an appointment. Best to you and the bride!" her message read.

Dr. John then entered Quinn's cell number and typed a message: "Call me as soon as possible!" He hit the send button and thought, *This is not good.*

———

LEVI SAT AT HIS DESK AND KNEW WHAT HE HAD TO DO next. He really needed to see Sue Ann's phone records. He realized that she would not use the department-issued phone to conduct any private business or anything that would get her in trouble.

He knew where he had to check first. His contact at US Cellular in Galax owed him a favor. Tyler Cary had gotten in a jam when he discovered his girlfriend was having an affair with another man.

Tyler found out who the other guy was and where he lived. Tyler went to the man's house and confronted him. He then beat the man up. It turned out that Levi knew the lover quite well and got all charges against Tyler dismissed.

Levi decided to drive to Galax and visit Tyler at the US Cellular office.

Tyler smiled when he saw Levi walk in. "If it isn't the best damn detective in all of southwest Virginia."

Levi smiled as they shook hands. "I might be the best detective in all of Virginia and maybe North Carolina as well!" Both men laughed.

"So, what brings you all the way from Hillsville to see me, brother?"

"This might come as a surprise to you, but I need your help. One of our own might have a phone from y'all, and I need to know if she does. That is the very first thing I need to know."

Tyler fired up his desktop. "Name please?"

"Sue Ann Kollman," Levi offered.

"No, that name isn't in our system. But wait—let me try some variations." He took a few minutes to type in all variations he could think of. Suddenly, he stopped. "Bingo. How about an AK Kollman at this address?"

Levi's eyes lit up. "Dang, you are good, brother. Can you dump the activity on that phone for me? You know I can get a warrant if I need to, but I'm in a hurry."

Tyler rolled his eyes. "How far back do you want?"

Levi frowned. "At least a year is needed."

Tyler looked at the screen and hit several keys. Levi could hear the printer in the office humming away. In a moment, Tyler went back to the office to retrieve the printout. He came back with a sealed envelope in his hand.

"Levi, you didn't get this from me. I will deny ever seeing you," Tyler offered as they shook hands.

Levi turned to leave, and as he got to the door Tyler spoke again, "One more thing, Levi, that I forgot to mention. There was another person listed on the account, and for the longest time, it seems he paid for it. Some fella named Tommie Cruz."

Levi stopped in his tracks. *"What the hell!"*

———

SANDY WINSTON GOT BACK TO HIS OFFICE AT THE HEADquarters building and closed the door. He fired up his computer and put in the name Yuri Dobrow. The screen came alive with pages of information.

It seemed that he was here on a legitimate work visa and had an import/export business in New York City as his address. As he read through more pages of the report, Winston saw there was some suspicion that Yuri was somehow connected to the Bratva, but no one could ever prove it.

He then looked up a number of someone he hadn't touched base with in some time. He dialed the number, and the answer came on the second ring. "I hope I'm not in trouble if the esteemed director of the Federal Bureau of Investigation is calling."

Winston laughed. "No, Lefty, you are as good as gold as far as I'm concerned, but of course that just might change."

Lefty Uzzell was a senior administrator in the Federal Aviation Administration. He had worked with Winston in the past on a few investigations.

"So, I am guilty as charged for not calling more often, but you do know that the phone you're holding calls both ways. How in the hell are you and your family?"

"You're right—we are both negligent when it comes to staying in touch. The family is, well, all grown up. I do like being an empty nester, though. Aren't you going to retire soon?"

"Not soon enough, my friend. I'm going to buy a place in the mountains and live happily ever after. Just a couple of years left. As you can imagine, I need a favor.

"I could have one of my agents find this out, but I thought it might be quicker if you could help. So, this is what I need: Last Saturday, a private helicopter picked someone up in Falls Church and took that person somewhere. I need to know where that somewhere is."

Uzzell paused. "Is that all? How about any moon landings on that day? Hey, sit tight. Let me query my super-duper computer to see what comes up. I would ask if you had a tail number, but I know better."

Several minutes passed before Uzzell came back on the line. "What is this information worth to you? Maybe a dinner at the Old Ebbitt Grill later this week?"

Winston laughed. "Deal. Let's have what you got."

"Let's see now. A private helicopter did land in Falls Church on Saturday. A flight plan was filed, and it traveled to its base in Carroll County, Virginia. Seems it's registered and owned by a religious group in some place called Pipers Gap, Virginia."

"Wow, I'm impressed. That is exactly what I needed. And one more thing: do let me know if and when that helicopter flies again. I guess you expect me to buy dinner?"

"My friend, you are spot on. Will Thursday night work?"

"It will indeed. See you on Thursday," Winston offered before he hung up.

He turned to his computer and typed in Pipers Gap, Virginia. As the images came to life, he smiled and thought to himself, *I know somebody who lives in that neck of the woods.*

He reached for his cell phone and looked up a number. Once he found it, he smiled when he saw her name on the screen . . . *Louisa Hawke.*

———

QUINN AND LOUISA WALKED INTO THE FANCY GAP DELI to grab a late lunch. They were both starved and needed a bite to eat. As they walked in, Sharon the manager waved at them. Once they were seated in their favorite corner booth, Sharon brought out two glasses of sweet tea.

Sharon looked at Louisa. "Girl, get up and give me a hug. I have missed you both, but in reality, I missed you more, Louisa, than that big hunk. But I'm here to tell you I did protect him from you-know-who, and that wasn't easy!"

All three burst into laughter as Louisa looked at Quinn with a big smile on her face. He held up one hand. "Truth be told, this tall, long-legged brunette was probably the one you needed to worry about. 'Cause everybody knows that Libby can't cook."

They laughed until tears welled up in their eyes.

"Okay, you two, I bet I know that you want what you usually have, right?"

Both Quinn and Louisa nodded in the affirmative. Just as she turned to leave, Quinn's phone buzzed. He looked down and saw Dr. John's name on the screen. He showed Louisa before he answered.

"You aren't going to spoil our lunch, are you? We're at the deli, and we're hungry."

There was pause on the other end. "Now you've got me thinking about food. But listen, and I'll make this quick: Your red blood cell count is way too high. There are a number of possibilities as to why that has happened.

"What you need to do is see a specialist in Winston-Salem. Dr. Jackson is well versed in all of these types of things. I gave her the basic info about you, and they are expecting your call to schedule an appointment.

"I know you're about to ask me a thousand questions, but don't. Dr. Jackson is the right person to answer your questions and deal with whatever you have to deal with. I'm going to text you her telephone number. Make the call, and do have a great lunch."

Before Quinn could say a word, the line went dead. He watched the screen on his phone as the text message from Dr. John came through. He looked at Louisa with a quizzical expression on his face. "He has referred me to a Dr. Jackson in Winston-Salem."

Louisa looked at him. "What does she do?"

"I don't know 'cause he didn't tell me."

Louisa took out her phone and brought up a browser page. She typed in Dr. Jackson's name with an office in Winston-Salem. She looked at her phone for the longest time.

Quinn finally asked, "Well, what does she do?"

Louisa hesitated for a moment. *"She is an oncologist."*

YURI DOBROW SAT IN HIS OFFICE AND KNEW WHAT HE had to do next. Sue Ann Kollman had identified Elena as the person who had handed the note to her. While he had a soft spot in his heart for Elena, he knew that her actions must be punished.

Only Anatoly Kristoff, his chief of security, knew of the breach. While Anatoly would expect some remedial action to be taken, he would understand if he decided not to impose any punishment.

Yuri was aware that Elena was a main cog in the wheel he had set for future visits. He was also aware that Ale Schumer, the powerful Democratic leader in the Senate, was going to be the next visitor in a couple of days.

He pushed a button on his desk phone. A phone rang in another building.

Elena was just getting back from the gym when she heard the phone ring in her room. She answered, "Hello."

The voice on the other end responded, "Elena, this is Yuri. Come to my office immediately."

Elena was taken back. "But of course, Yuri, I will be right there." She hung up the phone and tried to imagine why he would be calling. Perhaps he needed to have sex with her or something else was on his mind.

Within five minutes, she knocked on his door.

"Come in," was the reply on the inside.

She walked through the door and walked to the front of his desk. His back was to her, as he was typing on his computer. He never acknowledged her presence as he continued to type. She looked at the clock on the wall and realized that ten minutes had passed since she walked through the door.

Yuri finally tuned around and looked at her. "Sit on the couch."

She walked over and sat on the end of the couch. He stood from his desk, walked over, and stood right in front of her.

"Elena, are you happy here?" he asked.

She looked at him without smiling. "Yes, I am, Yuri. I am very happy."

He frowned. "Are you certain that you are happy? You wouldn't lie, would you?"

Elena started to feel uncomfortable sitting there. "Please understand that I am faithful to you and what we do here."

"No, Elena, I don't believe you are. Did you forget what happens if you do anything that would jeopardize what we do here? Let me refresh your memory. Your parents will both be killed, Elena. Do you want that to happen?"

Elena's mind raced through what might have happened to the note she passed to the woman police officer. She understood that police officers in the United States were honest and, unlike the police in Russia, did not accept bribes.

"Please, Yuri, I want no harm to come to my parents. I love them dearly, and I hope to see them ageing after my service is finished here. I couldn't live with myself if any harm would come to them."

Yuri turned and went to his desk, where he picked up two pieces of paper. He slowly returned to the couch. He looked at one of the pieces. He handed it to Elena.

She looked at it and held back tears.

"Read it to me, Elena."

She started to cry as she read, "Please help us. We are being held captive!" Tears rolled down her cheeks as she sat there.

Yuri handed her the second piece of paper. "Who is this, Elena?"

She started to cry harder. "This is the woman I gave the piece of paper to."

"So, you gave the paper to a police officer. You could see she was a police officer, couldn't you?"

Elena cried harder. "Yes, I could."

Yuri took both pieces of paper and set them on his desk. He turned and stood before her. "You lied to me. You aren't happy here, are you? Why would you do such a thing if you were happy? I don't understand."

Elena looked down to the floor.

Yuri shouted, "Look at me and keep looking at me! You must decide, Elena. I will kill one of your parents. Which one should it be? Should I kill your mother or your father?"

Elena fell to her knees in front of him. "I beg of you, please do not kill my parents. I will do anything you ask. Please do not kill them!" She sobbed uncontrollably as she spoke.

"Now you beg forgiveness for something you should have never done and you understand the consequences of your actions, don't you?"

She sobbed even harder as she held on to his legs. "I was a fool who deserves to be punished. But I beg you not to kill my parents. Kill me and do it right now, but please spare my parents."

Yuri didn't talk for a long time. The only sound in the room was Elena sobbing.

"Elena, I should kill you right now, as I should kill your parents as well. Your stupidity could have taken down all we worked so hard to put together. If I let you live, how can I come to trust you? What will stop you from talking to a guest who is here? How do I know you didn't encourage one of the other girls to say something or do something stupid?"

Elena looked at him with bloodshot eyes. "I never spoke of my actions to any of the other girls. I did not do that. I swear I didn't!"

Yuri backed off a step or two from where he was standing. "Stand up, turn around, and pull your gym shorts down."

Elena did as he asked.

"Now bend over on the couch."

She never saw him take off his leather shoe. He swung it back and struck her right buttock with the shoe. Elena gasped but didn't move. He swung back and hit her other cheek with his shoe. He continued until he had hit each cheek at least ten times. Elena bit down on her tongue as the pain intensified. When he stopped, he walked back to his desk and sat. She continued to look at the wall in front of her.

"Pull up your shorts and return to your room."

Elena reached down and pulled them up as she walked to the office door. She stopped at the door and turned to look at him. Before she could speak, he held his hand up.

"Not a word, and leave immediately before I decide to kill you!"

She opened the door and left. She passed Anatoly Kristoff, who was headed to Yuri's office. He walked in and looked at Yuri. "What have you decided to do with her?"

Yuri smiled. "Oh, I have plans for her . . . *very special plans.*"

———————

LEVI PULLED INTO THE CARROLL COUNTY SHERIFF'S Department parking lot. His mind still swirled around the information he had received in Galax. Not only was Sue Ann Kollman somehow associated with the killers who lived in Pipers Gap, she was now connected to Tommie Cruz.

He hurried up the stairs to his office. Once inside, he set down the call records for Sue Ann's personal phone. While most of the calls were in the local two-seven-six area code, he did not recognize any of the numbers. He went to his file cabinet and pulled out an investigative file. "Tommie Cruz" was printed at the top. He spread the contents out on his desk until he found what he was looking for.

The cell phone records for Cruz were part of the file. He finally found Cruz's personal number. He looked at Sue Ann's call records; the numbers matched. He set those documents to the side on his desk.

He then went online to look up the main number for the conference center in Pipers Gap. He compared that number to the records for Cruz and Kollman. In a moment, he realized that both Kollman and Cruz had called that number.

He sat back in his chair and digested what he now knew. It became clear to him that Sue Ann Kollman was very involved with Tommie Cruz. Yet he knew that while the whole Cruz investigation was going on, Kollman had been privy to many of the investigative details.

He now suspected that Cruz was somehow involved in whatever was going on at the religious conference center. He rubbed his forehead as he wondered just how deeply Sue Ann was involved in all of this.

He stopped for a moment as he saw the sheriff go into his office. He gathered the paperwork from his desk, stuffed it into a folder, and stuck it under his arm as he walked across the hall to the sheriff's office.

He peeked in the door and saw that the sheriff had just hung up his phone. "Leroy, we need to talk 'cause I got some shit that you need to be aware of."

The sheriff turned and looked at him. "I have seen that look before. Like a bloodhound getting close to the prey. Sit down and tell me what you found."

Levi sat and set the folder on the table. "I done found out some shit. I went to Galax and found Sue Ann's personal phone records. And you ain't gonna believe who she is connected to."

Levi paused for a long moment. The sheriff spoke up, "Do I get three guesses, or are you going to tell me?"

Levi grinned from ear to ear. "To begin, I believe she was Tommie Cruz's girlfriend."

The sheriff stiffened. "What? Tommie Cruz had another woman—what was her name? Wasn't it Missy or something like that?"

"You're sure nuff right, Leroy, that Missy was his main squeeze. But I believe that Sue Ann was his number two. He might have kept her 'cause she worked here and had access to a whole bunch of stuff."

"Levi, you now have to convince me that she was connected to Cruz."

Levi opened the folder, pulled out a few sheets of paper and laid them on the desk in front of the sheriff. "Take a gander at this, Leroy. This is the account that Sue Ann uses, and look at the bottom to see who paid for it."

The sheriff picked up the papers and examined them closely. It took him a moment to set them down. "By God, Levi, this is shocking! I would have never imagined Sue Ann of all people. And even while Cruz tried to kill me and Quinn McSpain, she never said a word."

Levi smiled. "And don't forget, Leroy, who took the shot that killed that sorry son of a bitch! Yes, I sure nuff did kill that monster!"

Leroy picked more of the files and read them. "So, I follow the lines you have drawn on these and see where Sue Ann called the conference center as well. So, she not only called them, she drove out there for some reason only known to her and the people out there she met with.

"This is all outrageous. I mean, we trust Sue Ann with our lives and believe she is honest and truthful. But now I don't know what to believe. This is insane."

"You're right, Leroy, this just ain't right. To think one of our own is on the other side of the law dealing with a madman who tried to kill us and now some kooky religious folks who killed and burned two innocent people!" Levi sat forward in his chair and looked at the sheriff. "So, what is our next move, Leroy? I'm chomping at the bit to sit her down and see what she has to say. I feel sick to my stomach 'cause I like Sue Ann, but she gotta go down if she's dirty. And It damn sure looks that way!"

The sheriff stood and looked out his window. He turned and looked at Levi. "We need to be careful and do this right. Sue Ann is smart. We need to get all of our ducks in order before we sit down with her.

"I'm dumbfounded with all of this, so I need to let all of this sink in before we take our next steps. Quite frankly, Levi, *all of this is making me sick!*"

CHAPTER 16

QUINN PAID THEIR LUNCH BILL AT THE DELI AND HUGGED
Sharon as they left. Not a word was spoken as they crossed
the parking lot and got into Quinn's truck. They looked
at each other for a moment.

Louisa was the first to speak. "Well, my dearest, I
guess there is no time like the present to make the call."

Quinn nodded and looked at his cell phone. He dialed the Winston-Salem number, and it rang for several
moments.

"Hello, this is Dr. Jackson's office. May I help you?"
the voice on the other end said.

"Yes, this is Quinn McSpain calling. I was referred to
Dr. Jackson by Dr. John in Fancy Gap, Virginia."

The voice on the other end paused. "Why, yes, Mr.
McSpain, we have been expecting your call. Please hold
for Dr. Jackson."

Quinn looked at Louisa, but before he could say anything, a voice came on the line. "Hello, Mr. McSpain, this is Dr. Jackson. I'm so pleased that you called so quickly. I spoke with Dr. John this morning about your symptoms.

"Please don't be alarmed because he referred you to an oncologist. I am a blood specialist as well, and what we need to do is run further blood tests on you so we can zero in what's happening with your elevated hematocrit. How soon can you come in to see me?"

Quinn cleared his throat. "I'm pretty flexible. How soon can you see me?"

"How about this afternoon at four o'clock? I've had a cancellation; can that work for you?" she asked.

"It certainly can, Dr. Jackson, and please do call me Quinn."

She laughed. "I will, Quinn, and see you at four o'clock."

Louisa heard most of the conversation and looked at Quinn. "Looks like we are going to Winston-Salem right now, aren't we?"

Quinn backed the truck out of the deli parking lot and headed south down the Highway 52 toward North Carolina. They were both silent as Quinn maneuvered through the twisting downhill turns that didn't end before they reached Cana at the bottom of the mountain.

Quinn looked at Louisa. "Do you know that Carroll County is unique because, while it is mostly comprised of mountain communities, it has a piedmont in Cana as well? That is very unusual."

Louisa looked at him. "Well now, Mr. Smarty-Pants, please do tell me something else I don't know."

Before Quinn could answer, Louisa's cell phone rang. She looked down at the screen and paused. "This is the second biggest surprise of my day. To what do I owe the honor of a call from the director of the Federal Bureau of Investigation?"

Sandy Winston laughed before he spoke. "Louisa, from time to time, those of us still employed as government bureaucrats worry about those lucky souls that got away and are hiding in the remote mountains of Virginia."

"Sandy, I couldn't be hiding all that well if you found me, now could I? Didn't I hear a rumor that you are about to retire—or was that just a rumor?"

"I have tried to retire three times. But you know I acquired a young wife some time ago who has expensive tastes and loves to travel. But I really do have a plan, and I'm gone in twelve months or so."

"Good for you. I'm here to tell you that I'm pleased I walked away when I did. And I hear you haven't been able to find another chief of the criminal division who is as good as I was."

He laughed before he spoke. "Listen, Louisa, I need your help. I do believe you are living in Fancy Gap with that handsome man you've been seen with. But what I need to know is, are you anywhere near some place called Pipers Gap?"

Louisa almost dropped her phone. Quinn was listening, as it was in speakerphone mode. "Yes, Sandy, we are. It's only about twenty-five miles from us. Why do you ask?"

"My dear friend, you didn't hear this from me, but someplace that looks like a religious conference center is not that at all. It seems that a very important someone from high on up the pecking order in the White House went out there a few days ago.

"I hear you thinking, *What did he just say?* You heard me right. That certain somebody went out there for twenty-four hours of pure erotic sexual adventures with seven of the most beautiful women on earth."

Quinn and Louisa looked at each other. "What did you just say, Sandy? Did I hear you right?"

"Oh, yes, you did. I saw a tape that was put together of the highlights of his visit there. And trust me, they were highlights."

Louisa cut in, "So a mucky-muck from the White House flies out to Pipers Gap to screw his brains out? Is that right?"

"Yes, Louisa, it is, and guess where the tape showed up? Well, let me tell you. The Russian ambassador shows up with it and tries to blackmail the guy with it!"

Louisa didn't talk for a moment. "Listen, Sandy. I am very close to the sheriff here in Carroll County. One of his deputies might just be involved with that group in some way, shape, or form. There were two people killed and burned in a cabin that might have been murdered by people related to the conference center."

Winston took a while to reply. "So, Louisa, on face value, it looks like some badass Russians are out there in the middle of nowhere trying to influence our government. That sound right?"

"It does, Sandy, it certainly does. Anything planned on your end yet?" Louisa asked.

"No, not at the moment, as I wanted to touch base with you first."

"I'm glad you did, Sandy. Let me suggest that I talk with the sheriff in the morning and get back to you after I do. Will that work?"

"It will, and I look forward to talking with you soon. Goodbye."

Quinn shook his head. "This is crazy. The Russians in our backyard? There is some interesting and important stuff going on here."

Louisa looked at him. "Not hardly as important *as the next two hours in Winston-Salem.*"

Senate Minority Leader Ale Schumer got caught up in traffic as he was crossing the bridge out of the District of Columbia heading into Virginia. He was late leaving the office and needed to be at the Leesburg Executive Airport in one hour.

He didn't want to be late, as the anticipation of spending twenty-four hours in some exotic place with beautiful women excited him. He also knew that the highest level of discretion was in play, so his privacy was ensured.

It had been two years since his wife of forty years had passed away. He failed miserably at socializing in the district or at home, where all his friends attempted to fix him up with women who didn't interest him.

The only interest he had was to deal with his sex drive, which hadn't diminished that much even as he'd aged. So, the opportunity to live out sexual fantasies appealed to him. In the back of his mind, he worried about what this sort of sexual exertion might have on his cardiac health.

Some three years past during a routine physical, his family doctor detected a cardiac murmur. He referred him to a cardiologist, who administered a series of tests to determine the case of the murmur.

The result, according to the cardiologist, was that his heart was suffering from aortic stenosis. The doctor explained that his aortic valve was narrowing. That narrowing prevented the valve from opening fully. That restricted the flow of blood to his body.

After a two-year period, he knew he was getting weaker and weaker. He tired when he walked up a flight of stairs. He knew it was time to see his cardiologist again.

More tests were administered, and the decision was reached that his aortic valve needed to be replaced. Soon thereafter, he met with a young cardiac surgeon, who gave his three options.

The first was have an artificial valve used to replace his worn-out aortic valve. The doctor advised that if he chose the artificial valve, he would be on blood thinners for the rest of his life. However, the artificial valve would never wear out. The next options were to have either a pig valve or a cow valve used. In the end, he chose the cow valve since the doctor thought it would best suit his size. The operation came shortly thereafter.

Since he maintained a heathy lifestyle, his recovery period was shorter than normal. He quickly was back to walking, and soon thereafter, he was riding his mountain bike. He was only on blood thinners for some thirty days after the operation.

The positive effects of the new valve were soon realized. His endurance levels quickly increased, and his overall health improved. He soon realized that the new cow valve also efficiently delivered blood to the part of his anatomy that he'd long considered in a retired state.

He thought of this as he pulled into the private parking area at the Leesburg Airport. He locked his car and walked toward the office area. Once he entered, he saw a tall man get up from where he was sitting and start walking toward him.

The man held out his hand. "Welcome, Senator, your helicopter is ready. Please follow me."

He smiled as they walked out the back door of the office and toward a white helicopter that had a large cross painted on the side. The man smiled as he opened the back door and motioned for the senator to step in.

The pilot smiled and waved at him as he sat down. The other man closed the back door and seated himself in front alongside the pilot. He felt a hand on his shoulder as a slender blond woman slipped between the seats and sat beside him.

He was immediately taken with her beauty. She smiled and reached into the small cabinet in front of her. She removed two chilled champagne flutes. She handed both of them to him before beginning to uncork the bottle. He recognized the bottle as an expensive French brand that he had enjoyed once before. Once the cork was removed, she poured some into his glass as well as into hers.

She leaned over and touched her glass to his. She smiled as she leaned close enough to whisper in his ear. "Senator, this will be the most exciting and memorable champagne you will ever enjoy."

She held her glass close to her lips and slowly licked the edge of her glass before she took a sip. He quickly took a sip as he felt his heart rate increase and sensed a stirring between his legs that he hadn't felt in a long time.

Once she had finished her second sip, she handed her glass to him. He held both of the glasses as she slowly started to unbutton her blouse. After her fingers finished with the fifth button, she seductively slipped the blouse down over her left shoulder. He was mesmerized as she brought her right hand over and let her index finger slip into his glass. In a slow moment, she withdrew it and brought it up to her now-exposed nipple.

She slowly let the champagne drip down as she massaged her breast. He felt small droplets of sweat on his forehead. He never realized the helicopter was already *airborne.*

———

SANDY WINSTON WALKED BACK TO HIS OFFICE. IT WAS midafternoon, and he was already worn out. The meeting in the human resources office he'd come from was unsettling.

Evidence was presented that a senior agent was accepting bribes from Hispanic mobsters in Los Angeles who managed a successful money laundering operation from proceeds extracted from a highly productive drug trafficking ring.

The investigative team had put together evidence that the agent in question had received over $300,000 in bribes. To his dismay, Winston knew the agent in question and was shocked by what had transpired.

He sat behind his desk and considered a trip to the locked cabinet in his personal closet. A sip or two of his favorite single-malt scotch would be most appropriate at that moment.

Just as he stood, his desk phone rang. He saw Lefty Uzzell's name on the screen. He picked up the phone. "So, do you want to change our dinner date, or are you offering to pay?"

The voice on the other end of the line chuckled. "Sandy, I'm going on a hunger strike on the day you're buying dinner. I want to be darn sure that I'm as hungry as I possibly can be when you're picking up the tab.

"Now with what I'm about to tell you, I suggest we order lobster and filet mignon when we dine. I hope you're sitting down. Since we discussed that helicopter you had an interest in, I put a tag on any activity it might be engaged in.

"It turns out that my tag sent an alert that the copter in question left Pipers Gap and flew all the way to the private airport in Leesburg. That got my attention. The airport manager at Leesburg is an old friend. I called him to see if he knew anything about that helicopter's presence at his airport.

"It turns out he was in his office when it landed, and when he went out to the lobby to get something, he stopped in his tracks when he saw that the helicopter was there to pick up someone very special." He paused for a moment before he continued, "I should really have you try to guess as to who the important person was who hitched a ride in that fancy copter. But since I really like you, my friend, I'll tell you.

"It was none other than Ale Schumer, our esteemed senate minority leader. I was taken back at first, but when I got a closer look, it certainly was Schumer who got on board.

"He went out on the tarmac to get a closer look and could see that besides the pilot, there was a man in the front seat as well as a woman sitting very close to ole Ale when it lifted off. Being the inquisitive person that I am, I tracked it right back to Pipers Gap, where it came from."

Winston looked out the window as he digested what he had just heard. "Listen, Lefty, you will get wined and dined. This was extremely valuable information. I give you credit, my friend, I owe you for all of this."

"Sandy, it was my pleasure. Glad I could help. Keep the faith, and I will see you on Thursday."

Winston hung up and considered his next move. He knew the president would relish this information, as he knew, as did all of Washington, that Schumer and the president did not get along well.

He took out his cell phone and dialed a number. Frank Stillhouse answered after three rings. "Sandy Winston calling me late in the afternoon. I'm surprised you're still there. Don't you fellas end your workdays at three in the afternoon? I mean, with golf and tennis, I'm surprised you don't leave before three."

Winston smiled, as he knew that Stillhouse knew of his reputation as a workaholic. He rarely left the office before seven in the evening. "I'm pleased that you're surprised as you are. Then again, I'm surprised I caught you in the office. Don't you have a regular appointment to get your pedicure at the Vietnamese nail salon?"

Both men laughed at their comments.

"Now, Frank, is the president in his office?"

"You are in luck! I'm headed in there for a meeting with him in five minutes. Do you want to talk with the both of us or just the president?"

"The both of you would be great. Call me when you can; I'll stay in my office and wait for your call." He hung up the phone and stood.

He was somewhat surprised that Schumer was involved in this mess at all. While he didn't like Schumer's politics, he respected him for a number of reasons. In the past, Schumer had risen above his own party and politics to deal with a member of his party who was a pedophile. Others within the leadership of the party had urged him to support the senator, but Schumer knew the man was sick and needed to be treated for his mental illness.

At the end of the day, the senator resigned and entered a psychiatric hospital for treatment. Schumer was later privately applauded by his peers for his bipartisan approach to the problem.

The sound of Winston's phone ringing startled him for a moment. He saw that the president was calling. He picked up the phone. "Gentlemen, a good afternoon to you."

President Rogers spoke, "Sandy, we're both here. What have you got for us?"

"I'm here to report that the white helicopter with the cross on the side has flown again. It seems it left Pipers Gap and flew to the private airport in Leesburg. It picked up its passenger and immediately departed for the return trip to Pipers Gap.

"And the man in the rear passenger seat was none other than . . . *Ale Schumer!*"

———

THE TRIP TO WINSTON-SALEM SEEMED SHORTER THAN usual. Quinn and Louisa bantered back and forth on different theories as to why the Russians had set up shop in Pipers Gap of all places. They agreed that whoever was behind the effort spared no expense in building the complex.

They were also surprised that no red flags whatsoever had become apparent as the whole process began from beginning to end. Louisa surmised that the Carroll County leaders were ecstatic that such a conference center was built in their poor and rural county. Needless to say, any possible irregularities were ignored or swept under the rug.

The entire question as to what Sue Ann Kollman had to play in all of it led them both down several avenues of possibilities.

Quinn looked at Louisa. "For the life of me, I can't fathom why Sue Ann is involved in any of this. She has always been a treat to work with on any of the adventures we have endured up here."

"I agree, Quinn. She is the last person on earth I would have thought could collude with Russians of all people. Yet, what do we really know of Sue Ann? Heck, I don't know if she has ever had a boyfriend—or a girlfriend, for that matter. I don't know if she hunts or fishes or whatever she does in her free time."

"Exactly, Louisa, we simply took her for granted. I wouldn't expect us to get to know all the folks in the sheriff's department, but sometimes I guess we are a bit superficial in our relationships with people we come into contact with."

"Just wait a minute—exactly what are you saying? We came together to live in a beautiful slice of paradise and enjoy a quiet life together. But just take a look back on our years here in Fancy Gap.

"We first get involved with a crazy priest who tried his best to kill us. And, by golly, he almost did. Then we went head-to-head with our young terrorist who had us all fooled while she created her deadly genetically modified corn seed that, indeed, did kill people.

"And then to top things off, along comes the Mexican drug cartel bad guys who were hell-bent on eradicating the entire Mennonite population in Carroll County. So, I thought we were on our way to peace and quiet until the Russians, of all people, show up in our backyard.

"Is that all crazy, or is it just me?"

Louisa reached over and patted him on his cheek. "My dearest, we got through all of that, and we will get through the Russians as well. Now if you would please pay attention, as you need to turn on University Parkway coming up here on the right, as we have arrived in Winston-Salem."

Quinn looked over at his navigation system display, which indicated the turn-by-turn directions to get them to the Novant Health Davis Cancer Center. They soon found themselves turning off Hawthorne Road into the cancer center parking lot.

He pulled the Ram into a parking spot and turned off the engine. They sat in silence for a moment before Louisa leaned over and kissed him. He could see a tear rolling down her cheek.

"Okay, my badass girlfriend, let's get in there and see what has decided to take up residence in this perfect temple of mine and see what needs to be done."

She took his hand and squeezed. "Whatever the outcome of all of this, you know I will be by your side."

Quinn tugged at his door handle and looked at her. "Let's get inside and meet some new folks."

Louisa smiled as she opened her door and slid out. They walked slowly to the front entrance as several patients were leaving the building.

A bald woman with deep circles under her eyes smiled at them as she passed. She was supported on her husband's arm. Several more patients in wheelchairs passed them as they approached the reception desk.

The woman smiled as Quinn provided her with his name and date of birth. She recorded all of his Medicare and United Healthcare information. When she was finished, she looked at Quinn. "Dr. Jackson has requested that your blood be drawn before she sees you. Just go around the corner to the waiting area one. Thank you, and all the very best."

Quinn smiled back and walked hand-in-hand with Louisa to the waiting area. The room was almost full with over twenty patients waiting. They sat and took in the surroundings. It quickly became apparent to them both that they were surrounded by some very sick people.

A tall man wearing a volunteer vest was walking around the room with a cart full of water and coffee. He stopped once he got to Quinn and Louisa and smiled at them both. Quinn smiled as he accepted a bottle of water from the man. Louisa opted for a cup of coffee.

The man looked at Quinn. "Are you the patient?"

Quinn looked at him. "Why, yes, I am."

The man asked, "Here for blood work or chemo?"

Quinn replied, "Just blood work today."

The man reached down and patted his hand. "That's good, young man, it shouldn't be too long before they call you."

They both smiled back at him as he walked off. Louisa looked at Quinn. "Young man? Exactly who was he looking at, I wonder?"

Quinn almost spit out the sip of water he had just taken. "That was a pleasant and very perceptive man, if I do say so myself."

They both chuckled under their breath.

The next voice they heard was from a woman who entered the waiting area: "Mr. Quinn McSpain."

Louisa gave his hand a squeeze as he stood. He smiled at her as he followed the technician into the room she was heading to. Once inside, she pointed to a chair for him to sit in.

Quinn looked around and counted three other patients sitting with technicians. He fidgeted a bit as the woman he was seated in front of reviewed the paperwork in front of her.

She finally looked at him. "Is your name Quinn McSpain?"

Quinn smiled, "Why, yes, it is, thank you."

She gave him a stern look. "Well, Mr. McSpain, my name is Dorothy but not the Dorothy from *The Wizard of Oz.* You're a big strapping man who would tell me if you were afraid of needles, wouldn't you?"

Quinn didn't immediately answer but felt the first drop of sweat on his forehead. "Dorothy, to tell you the truth, needles aren't my thing and never have been. But you look like you know what you're doing, so I won't worry so much."

Dorothy smiled. "Quinn—I hope you don't mind if I call you Quinn—it's been a busy day here already, and I am getting tired, and when that happens, I get the shakes."

Quinn started to get a bit faint as she cleaned off his arm with an alcohol swab. She then tied a rubber band around his arm. In the next instant, she reached over for the needle she needed to insert into his vein.

She smiled as she gently inserted the needle into his vein. Quinn flinched a bit and started to sweat more profusely. She could tell that he was uncomfortable. "That didn't hurt, did it?"

Quinn didn't say a word as she filled several vials full of his blood. After she filled the fourth one, she slipped the needle out and placed a small piece of gauze over the needle hole. She then took Quinn's finger and placed it upon the gauze.

"That wasn't so bad, was it?" she asked.

Quinn watched her take blue elastic tape, which she wrapped around the piece of gauze. He finally spoke: "I must admit that you were as smooth as silk with that needle. So, what happens now?"

Dorothy looked over his paperwork. "Well, young man, your blood will undergo a complete test, and the results will be sent to Dr. Jackson. Have you met her yet?"

"No, I haven't, but she comes highly recommended."

Dorothy shook her head. "She is the best at what she does. No matter what ails you, she is the gal to take care of you. And she is very easy on the eyes, if ya know what I mean.

"Now go back to the waiting room, get that beautiful woman you came in with and walk your way to waiting area two That is where Dr. Jackson is and take care of yourself, ya hear!"

Quinn smiled and blew her a kiss as he left. He closed the door and saw that Louisa was now surrounded by even more patients who had checked in. She stood as he approached.

"Pretty fancy arm band you have there. I guess you survived your encounter with the dreaded needle. But you do look a bit pale, my dearest."

Quinn took her hand as they headed to waiting area two. "You would have been proud of me. That wonderful woman who drew my blood didn't even see me cry like a baby. Came close, I must say, but we got her done!"

Louisa squeezed his hand, as she knew he hated any sort of needles. She had even thought he might pass out in the room he was in. "I'm proud of you. I didn't hear you scream or yelp in there."

They walked hand-in-hand down the corridor until they reached waiting area two. The room was about half full of patients. They smiled at the ones closest to them as they sat.

A television monitor on the wall was on, and a piece on breast cancer was playing. The interior door opened, and a nurse came out and called a name. A woman sitting across from them got up and followed the nurse into the next area.

Louisa looked at Quinn. "What do you think happens now?"

Quinn patted her on her knee. "Well, I bet that as we speak, my blood is being tested every which way it can be tested. I understand that they have some very sophisticated testing equipment here that will detect and diagnose just about anything going on in your blood. I think that once it finishes with the testing, a report is sent to my Dr. Jackson."

"Aren't you Mr. Smarty-Pants. I guess today's testing equipment has come a long way. So, we will certainly know a lot more about you and your blood in short order."

Quinn shook his head back and forth but stopped as the door opened and the nurse came out. "Mr. Quinn McSpain."

Quinn smiled as he and Louisa stood and headed toward the nurse. She smiled and held the door open for them both.

She led them to an electronic scale in the corner of the office. "Okay, Mr. McSpain, my name is Reem, and I need your date of birth please?"

Quinn obliged her with the dates.

"Thank you, and if you will please step up on the scale for me."

Louisa bent a bit forward to see the digital readout on the scale. The numbers stopped at 230 pounds. Louisa repressed a giggle as Quinn stepped off the scale.

Quinn looked at the nurse. "Reem, I think you need to have that scale checked because I just can't be that heavy!"

The nurse laughed. "Well, Mr. McSpain, that scale is brand new and we just calibrated it."

Louisa laughed. "Don't pay attention to him. He is too heavy, and he knows it."

Quinn held up his right hand. "I have to be light, as I just gave up ten gallons of blood in the other room."

They all laughed as Reem led them into an examining room. They all sat, and Reem opened the screen on her computer. She went through the perfunctory questions concerning his health, medications, and insurance.

Once all the information was entered, she took Quinn's blood pressure and temperature. She looked at the blood pressure cup then at Quinn. "Is your blood pressure always high?"

Quinn looked at Louisa. "Only when Louisa is in the room."

Reem laughed. "It isn't crazy high, but I'm sure Dr. Jackson will address that with you." She stood and offered, "Dr. Jackson will be with you shortly."

After the door closed, Louisa looked at Quinn. "That's another thing I didn't realize about you. How long has your blood pressure been high?"

Quinn frowned. "Well, like, forever. Inherited that trait from my mother. She had wicked high blood pressure all of her life and never took any medication to reduce it. Must I remind you that she lived till she was ninety-five years old? So, my dearest, I'm good to go for another thirty years or so. And, smarty pants, how high is your blood pressure?"

Before Louisa could answer, the door cracked open. "Is it safe to enter?" a female voice asked. Dr. Jackson slowly entered the room and introduced herself to both of them.

She sat in the chair behind the desk next to Quinn. "I'm pleased that you're both here today to see me. Dr. John and I talked at length, and he gave me the Reader's Digest condensed version of all the exciting things you get yourselves into up there in Fancy Gap."

She turned and sat closer to Quinn. "I'm certain that you know why Dr. John referred you to me. The simple blood test he performed indicated that your hematocrit or red blood cell count was dangerously high. That is never good, as the possibilities of blood clots get higher and higher as your blood thickens. My job is to find our why your hematocrit is bouncing off the ceiling. We are concerned about a range of possibilities with a host of worst-case possibilities.

"The blood that was taken from you today was tested by some very sophisticated equipment. As a result, I'm pleased to tell you that you don't have leukemia.

However, you do have something else that is causing the increases in your red blood cells. What you do have, Quinn, is a rare form of blood cancer called polycythemia vera or, as we call it, PV. You undoubtedly have never heard of this blood cancer because so few people in the United States have it. Estimates are that only some 100,000 or so folks have PV.

"What's happening in your body is that your bone marrow is working overtime in producing red blood cells. This is happening all day and night.

"I know what you are thinking. Unfortunately, modern medicine doesn't have a clue as to why you're one of the chosen few. And to make matters worse, there is no cure at this time. There is a major pharmaceutical firm working on developing another drug to treat PV, but that's about it.

"Accordingly, the most effective way of treating your polycythemia vera is with a chemo drug called hydroxyurea. What this drug does is attack your bone marrow, and that reduces the production of red blood cells. Hydroxyurea has been around for a lot of years and has proven to be effective in treating PV."

Dr. Jackson stopped talking and looked at them both. "Quinn, I know that's a lot to digest, but it is what it is. Questions?"

Quinn took a long breath and looked at Louisa. "I guess if I understand you right, I'm fortunate to not have something worse than this PV or whatever it's called. Yet I'm a bit dumbfounded by the fact that modern medicine is without any answers as to where it comes from and, more importantly, there is no cure. If I hear you right, I need to take this hydroxyurea for the rest of my life? Is that right?"

Dr. Jackson shook her head. "That's right, Quinn, or at least to some point in time when a cure is discovered."

Louisa leaned forward in her chair. "I'm trying to digest all of this as well. I'm not a rocket scientist, Dr. Jackson, but it seems that Quinn is in a very small pool of humans who have this polycythemia vera. So, my deduction at his point is what would be the financial reward for a drug company to spend millions trying to find a cure if there are so few folks with the problem?"

"Louisa, that is an excellent point. We are fortunate that hydroxyurea does and will probably work for Quinn. The drug company that is working on it is spending a lot of money on their efforts. I, for one, am convinced that they are in it for the long haul. I am very optimistic.

"Quinn, since your numbers are so high today, I suggest that it will be wise that we reduce the volume of blood in your system. I have set up a time for you this afternoon to have at least a pint of your blood drawn. That will ensure that the hydroxyurea has a better chance at being effective from the very beginning."

Quinn squirmed a bit in his chair. "Doc, do you use needles or leeches, like they did in the old days? I ask because I have no particular love for needles being in my arm for any great length of time."

Louisa smiled. "What he means is that this large macho man sitting in the chair across from you is scared silly of needles."

Quinn cringed again as Dr. Jackson stood. "Not to worry, Quinn, the nurses in the chemo center are some of the best. And I'm going to put in a special request just for you."

Quinn and Louisa looked at each other as Dr. Jackson got to the door. She smiled as she looked at Quinn. "*I just know they can find a sharp needle just for you.*"

———

ALE SCHUMER FELT THE HELICOPTER TOUCH DOWN AS the woman who was sitting beside him removed the hood over his head. His eyes quickly adjusted to the light, and he looked at the woman next to him.

She smiled as she leaned over and whispered, "Ale, I hope you enjoyed the trip we shared."

Schumer smiled from ear to ear. "My dearest, that was exquisite. You possess a rare talent that I greatly appreciated. I only hope we can meet again!"

She reached over, rubbed his crotch, and smiled. "I wouldn't miss your return trip for anything."

He turned as the passenger door next to him opened. He stepped out and was greeted by a man who was smiling.

"Senator Schumer, welcome! My name is Yuri, and I am so very pleased that you are with us."

Ale tucked his shirt back in his pants before he replied, "Well, Yuri, I can't imagine just how much better than the trip over was."

Yuri led him off of the landing pad toward the seven women, who were all smiling. He stopped at the first girl. "Ale, this is Elena, and she will be the first to show you around."

Elena stepped forward and gave him a kiss on the cheek. As Yuri introduced him to the six other girls, Ale was mesmerized with the pristine and angelic beauty of each.

Ale followed Yuri and Elena into what appeared to be a reception area.

Once inside, Yuri stopped and turned. "Now, Ale, I will give you Elena, who will take you on the next part of your twenty-four hours with us. I know you will not be disappointed."

Elena took his hand as Yuri left the room. She then led him into a grotto-like room filled with pools and waterfalls. Without saying a word, Elena sat him down in a velvet throne-like chair. She smiled as she spoke,

"There will be nothing better than a warm bath after your journey today."

Ale didn't reply as she kneeled before him and slid his shoes off. She slowly massaged his feet and his lower legs.

Her effort began to excite him. That increased as she slipped off her blouse and rubbed his foot in a circle around her firm and ample breast. Ale closed his eyes and thought, *Am I in heaven?*

LEROY SAT AT HIS DESK AND LOOKED OUT THE WINDOW. He was still in disbelief about Sue Ann Kollman. In all of his time as sheriff or any other of his years in the department, he did not know of anyone who wore the badge and went bad.

He realized that many of his deputies had financial challenges due to the lower-than-average salary he could pay the new staff members. The men and women who at times drank too much or gambled more than they should would never think of crossing over the line.

Sue Ann had never complained about financial challenges or anything else he could think of. He always considered her one of the best deputies. She was in line to be promoted to sergeant. All of this was so out of character for her. There was nothing he could think of that stuck out as any sort of red flag.

Levi knocked on his office door before entering. He sat in the chair facing Leroy. "Okay, I believe it's time we sit her down and confront her. And before you suggest that we need help from some investigator from the Virginia State Police, I'll suggest that we need to clean our own laundry."

The sheriff looked at Levi. "Exactly who do you suggest questions her? We don't have a female detective. And you know that normal protocol is we use an outside investigator to deal with potential illegal activities by any member of this department."

Levi was silent for a moment. "I understand that, Leroy, but there has to be a way to let us take a shot at this without outside involvement. Let us get more of the facts before having those dingbats from the state police mess things up."

"Levi, I believe we don't have a choice. The press will tear us apart if we don't go by the book on this one. We will look like idiots. Please call one of your contacts with the state police, and let's set things up."

Leroy could tell that Levi was upset. He watched Levi slowly get up from the chair and walk toward the door. He got halfway there before he stopped and turned. "Okay, Leroy, I just thought of an option."

The sheriff sat forward in his chair. "What do you suggest?"

Levi took three steps forward before he stopped. "Oh, Leroy, we do indeed have a resource we can use, and a damn good one at that. Right here under our noses, we have a resource.

"What we need to do is have Louisa Hawke question her. I know Sue Ann respects her, and hell, Louisa is a professional. We couldn't do no better."

Leroy swiveled around in his chair and looked out the window again. After a minute or so, he turned and looked at Levi. "Frankly, Levi, I just don't know if she would even want to get involved. Do you know how much we have asked from Louisa Hawke and Quinn McSpain over the past several years?

"I know you darn well know, and we both know how much of themselves they've given to help us. And you know that Louisa just returned from a stressful trip where she needed to figure some things out. While I'm sure she would probably be the best recourse we could have to question Sue Ann, I'm having a time trying to convince myself to ask her."

Levi walked up closer to the sheriff and put his arm around his shoulder. "Relax a bit, Leroy, *'cause I'll ask her.*"

QUINN LOOKED AT THE ROAD AHEAD AS THEY LEFT Winston-Salem heading north on Highway 52 toward Fancy Gap. He felt strange, as he wasn't driving. Louisa was behind the wheel of his Ram and had been since they left the cancer center.

He became weak about halfway through the process when his blood was being drawn. He felt sick to his stomach as he watched his blood drip into the bag hanging by his side.

The nurse who was drawing his blood quickly recognized the symptoms and gave him some soda to drink as well as a few cookies to eat. That helped to a degree but didn't make him feel much better.

He saw the faces of so many men and women patients who were in the large circular open space where chemo drugs were administered to so many. The look of anguish and despair on so many of the faces left a lasting impression. He was amazed by the many precautions the nurses took to protect themselves from the drugs they were charged to gently provide to those so ill.

Louisa looked over as she drove and could tell that Quinn was deep in thought. "My hunk of a man, I hope you're feeling a little better by now?"

Quinn looked at her. "I am, but I just can't stop seeing all of those terribly sick people who were in that room with us. I couldn't help but think that I was probably the healthiest patient in that room. Good Lord, that was a sobering experience."

Louisa kept on driving and looked straight ahead. "Quinn, I prayed for all of those poor souls today. So many women who had lost all their hair, and the ashen faces that still managed a smile at us as we passed by.

"But I also thought of you, Quinn McSpain, as you sat there. I do believe you are blessed to have all of this discovered when it was. I truly believe Dr. Jackson can and will be the resource that will be there for you. She knows her stuff, and I will make darn sure you follow her instructions."

Quinn reached over and patted her on the shoulder as she drove. "My dearest, my only immediate concern is that you are driving my truck, and while I love you dearly, I hate it when anyone but me drives my Ram."

They started to laugh and smile, which was interrupted by the chime of Louisa's phone ringing. She reached over and pushed the speakerphone button. They both saw the sheriff's name on the display panel.

Quinn was the first to talk: "Leroy, why in the world are you calling my girlfriend? I can only imagine and probably should hang up right this moment."

The voice on the other end replied, "Exactly where are you two? It's probably better that I talk with you both. I have Levi with me on my office speakerphone, and I'm calling you against my better judgement."

There was a pause before Levi spoke, "He's right—I came up with the bright idea to call you two. And he certainly did object, but in the end, he agreed that this is some thing we need to run by you, Louisa."

Louisa frowned as she drove. "My common sense tells me to hang up right now. But my enquiring mind tells me to at least listen to what you have to say."

"Well, Louisa," Leroy offered, "I really do hate to get you both involved in anything again. You have been so generous with your time in the past, but this is something where you could be of great assistance to us.

"As you know, we need to question Sue Ann, and question her soon. Under normal circumstances, I would call in a state police resource, preferably a female investigator to properly interrogate Sue Ann. But in the interim, I'm considering another preliminary course of action.

"I know that Sue Ann has immense respect for you. So, what I'm suggesting is that you and Levi sit down with her tomorrow and start the process. That gives us the opportunity to wash our own laundry for a bit until we discover the extent of her criminal activity.

"I know that's a lot to ask, Louisa, but I just had to run it by you. I would fully understand if you tell me to take a hike on this one. But I still have to ask."

Louisa glanced over at Quinn as she drove. He gave her a quizzical look. She looked forward again. "Leroy, my very first thought is to agree with you that a state police resource would be the way to go. Keeps things clean and above future reproach.

"But then on the other hand, I'm very curious as what the Russians are up to here in Pipers Gap, and Sue Ann might have a lot of the answers. I might just hate myself for doing this, but I think I can help with this one.

"Listen, you two, this is the very last time you can ever ask me or Quinn sitting here beside me to help on whatever mayhem comes your way in Carroll County. When do we need to get this done?"

Levi spoke up, "She comes in tomorrow morning. If you can be here by nine o'clock, that would be great."

Louisa reached over and pushed the off button on her phone. She looked at Quinn, who spoke, "Heck, do you think those two knew you are . . . *driving my Ram?*"

CHAPTER 17

PRESIDENT ROGERS LOOKED AT HIS WATCH. IT WAS FOUR thirty in the afternoon, and his calendar was clear for the rest of the day. He picked up his phone, hit the intercom button, and punched in Frank Stillhouse's number.

The phone rang twice before Stillhouse answered, "Yes, Mr. President, what's up?"

"Frank, come on down the hall. I need to run something by you," he said before he hung up.

Two doors down the hall, Frank Stillhouse looked at the chief of the Central Intelligence Agency, who was sitting across from him. They had just started a meeting. Stillhouse threw up his hands. "Raymond, looks like this meeting is over. I gotta go down the hall."

His visitor smiled and stood. "Better you than me." The two shook hands, and the chief turned and left the office. Frank checked his calendar and saw that his next appointment was an hour away.

Within a minute, he was at the door of the Oval Office. He knocked and heard the president respond, "Come on in, Frank, we have work to do."

Stillhouse walked over and sat in front of the President, who was looking out the large window in front of him.

"Ya know, Frank, I am one lucky son of a bitch to be standing in this office. Hell, no one expected the American public to reelect me after my first term. No sirree bob, all of the loyal opposition bet I wouldn't make it through the first term at all. All the impeachment bluster was all bullshit, I tell ya. But we showed 'em, didn't we, Frank? We just kicked their ass!"

Stillhouse sat and didn't say a word. He had witnessed the president's tirades from time to time and knew they usually were short-lived. "You're right, Mr. President, they missed all the signals from the American people. The folks out there truly love you, and they will continue to do so. You're more popular now than ever. Heck, we should consider changing the laws so you can run a third time!"

Both men laughed at that comment.

The president sat at his desk and looked at Frank. "It's time to call Ale Schumer and see if he's enjoying himself. He needs to know that we know exactly what he's up to."

With that, he picked up his personal cell phone and searched for the number. He stopped when he found the one he was looking for. He pushed the send button and saw Ale Schumer's name on the screen.

Meanwhile, some 333 miles away, Frank Stillhouse was pleasantly entwined between Natalia and Elena. He was completely lost in the gentle gyrations of the moment.

The sound of the distinctive ringtone that were coming from his cell phone finally got his attention. This ringtone was only assigned to one person, the president of the United States. Both girls were startled when his phone rang.

He slowly slid off the bed and walked over to the nightstand, where his clothes were neatly folded. He debated answering the call. Yet he understood that the president wouldn't call to check on the weather.

Both girls looked at him as he answered, "Hello, Mr. President, now what's going on that I have the pleasure of the president calling me?"

The president laughed before he answered, "I'm in the room with Frank Stillhouse, and we need to ask you something."

Schumer paused before he answered, "And what that be?"

"Well, Ale, I need to know if those beautiful young ladies you are with are fucking your brains out?"

Schumer was taken back *and dropped the phone.*

———

Quinn and Louisa sat at the breakfast table looking at each other. Quinn had put together some blueberry pancakes, which were stacked in front of them. When they'd returned from Winston-Salem, they had spent a quiet night and had gone to bed earlier than they normally did.

He took his fork and slid three pancakes over to his plate. His knife carefully placed small pads of butter between the pancakes before he smothered them with maple syrup. "This is exactly what I need this morning to get my mojo back. I'll admit I was a little weak last night. But don't forget, I was a whole pint down, you understand. So, these carbs are just what the doctor ordered."

Louisa took one pancake and placed it on her plate. She took the fruit bowl and smothered the pancake with strawberries and blueberries. She took her first bite as she watched Quinn devour his three pancakes.

He looked at her. "Louisa, I know that look. You are all concerned about what we heard yesterday. Rest assured, I am as well. But I do believe this PV thing is manageable. Exercise, good nutrition, and the medication she prescribed will do the trick. I just know it!"

She took a sip of orange juice before she replied, "You are always so positive and sure of yourself, Quinn

McSpain. Not all of us mortal human beings share your optimism."

"You should, Louisa, because I'll tell you why I feel good about this. Hell, at least I know what the challenge is. Yesterday I didn't know that. That's half the battle, I'm telling you. I can deal with what I'm aware of. I believe this is manageable. I really do."

Louisa looked at the kitchen clock. "Eat up, big man. It's time to get to the sheriff's office. I believe we're in for another interesting day."

Quinn stood and took the plates to the sink. "I'll do the dishes while you take your shower."

Within the hour, they were parking at the sheriff's office. They looked at each other as Quinn leaned over and kissed Louisa. "I believe you are the right person to talk with Sue Ann."

They walked hand-in-hand up the stairs to the sheriff's department.

Levi was the first to see them come in. He jumped up and walked over to hug Louisa and shake Quinn's hand. "Listen, you two, you don't how much this means to me. I really do believe this is the right way to approach this."

Louisa smiled as they walked into Leroy's office. He hung up his phone as they entered. He went over and hugged Louisa. "You know how much this means to us. I can never thank you enough."

Once they all sat down, Levi spoke. "Our plan is to bring Sue Ann into the interrogation room at nine thirty—this is in about ten minutes. She doesn't have a clue. I think the element of surprise will work in our favor."

"I agree," Louisa offered. "I assume you'll take the lead, Levi?"

He nodded his head in the affirmative. "I sure will, and I know you'll pick your moments to jump in. I just hope she cooperates with us."

The sheriff looked at his watch. "I believe it's time to get going. I'll get her and bring her in to you."

They all stood, and Louisa and Levi headed to the interrogation room.

The sheriff looked at Quinn. "I'll come back to the office after I bring her to the room. We can watch what's happening from the feed on my computer." He didn't close the door as he headed to Sue Ann's cube.

She was working on a report when he approached her. She looked up and smiled. "Good morning, Sheriff," she offered.

"Good morning, Sue Ann, would you come with me please."

Her smile disappeared as he led her to the interrogation room. He opened the door and led her in. She was startled to see Levi and Louisa in the room.

The sheriff motioned for her to sit. "Sue Ann, Levi and Louisa need to talk with you. I expect your full co-operation with them. Do you understand?"

Sue Ann blushed. "Of course, Sheriff, but what is this all about? Have I done something wrong?"

"Sue Ann, you are about to find out exactly what we need to know. Again, please be forthcoming!" He looked at the other two and left the room.

Levi adjusted his chair. "Sue Ann, understand that this is an interview and not an interrogation. I'm not going to read you your rights 'cause I don't have to. But I do expect you to be truthful."

Sue Ann nodded. "Levi, I'll try to be as truthful as I can. I don't believe I have anything to hide."

"That's good, Sue Ann, 'cause we need you to be truthful. My very first question is do you know anything about that religious compound in Pipers Gap?"

That question sent a jolt of electricity through her body. She already could feel the beads of sweat forming in her armpits. "I guess I know about as much as the next person. I read about it in the newspaper. I don't believe I know anything else about them."

Levi scribbled a few notes on the notepad in front of him. He stood and walked a little closer to her. "Sue Ann, think really hard. Have you ever visited that particular compound? Remember, I don't need you to be lying to me. We need the truth."

Sue Ann squirmed in her seat and thought before she replied, "Look, Levi, I'm not going to bullshit you. You already know I visited that place, or you wouldn't have me in here for questioning. I'm not fucking stupid."

"So, you did visit there, didn't you?" he asked. "Exactly why did you go there?"

She tensed up a bit. "If I went there, it is my own goddamn business and none of yours, Blackburn!"

Levi retuned to his chair and sat. "Well, ya see, Sue Ann, it is our business that you went there. This is because we know the Russians are running that place and they are up to no good. That presents a problem for you, young lady, because you had no legitimate business being there. That leads me to believe that you are somehow in cahoots with those Russkies. Fess up, Sue Ann, and tell us exactly what you were doing there."

She sat back and stared at Levi. "Fuck you, Levi, 'cause I ain't telling you jack shit. Do you understand, not a goddamn thing, you jackass!"

Levi smiled. "Sue Ann, I didn't know you held me in such high esteem. But that's not all I got for you. Tell us about your relationship with Tommie Cruz. Were you his girlfriend or something? I know he paid your phone bills."

Sue Ann stood up straight in her chair and stared down at Levi. "You mean the man you killed in cold blood! You mean that Tommie Cruz? You just couldn't leave well enough alone, could you? I hate you, Levi Blackburn! And I'm not saying another word to you!"

Levi looked at Louisa. She moved in closer to Sue Ann. "Sue Ann, I'm going to ask Levi to leave the room so we can talk." Louisa could tell that Levi was reluctant to leave.

He stood and smiled at Sue Ann as he turned to leave but stopped in his tracks. He turned and looked at Sue Ann. "I'll be needing your service pistol."

Sue Ann removed it from her holster and set it on the desk. Levi walked over and picked it up. "You won't be needing this anymore, Kollman."

She flipped him the bird as he left the room.

Louisa stood and changed chairs, now sitting much closer to Sue Ann. She slowly slid both of her hands across the table and took hold of Sue Ann's hands. She could feel Sue Ann's hands start to tremble.

Neither spoke for the longest time. Sue Ann slowly shifted her gaze to look directly at Louisa. Tears streamed down her cheeks as she spoke, "Louisa, I have really fucked up. I know that I have betrayed the trust of all of you, and there is no excuse for that."

Louisa reached over for the tissue box and slid it in front of Sue Ann. Louisa waited a moment while Sue Ann blew her nose. "Sue Ann, none of us are perfect. I know I have disappointed many in my life. I recently disappointed Quinn, the love of my life, and I never thought

I would ever do that. But I did. I was stupid and so out of character. After I did it, I was in the lowest of low places. I, quite frankly, never thought I would escape the guilt I was so laden with. But things did find a way to help me see the light and got me back here where I belong.

"Sue Ann, we won't hate you for what you did. We all have forgiveness in our hearts. Someday, you will look back on this day and wonder how you survived. But I'm confident that you will—I truly am."

Sue Ann dabbed her eyes with a tissue. "Louisa, you are a strong woman. You take charge of things and are confident in yourself. Hell, I'm just a country bumpkin who has nowhere to go. Sure, I have a good job here at the sheriff's department, but I wanted more.

"That's what Tommie Cruz promised me. I know he wasn't perfect, but he really loved me. He took care of me and showed me things I would have never seen with another man. I know he had another woman that he screwed. But I really didn't care 'cause he taught me to love other women as well.

"My heart is still broken over the fact that Tommie is dead. I blame that asshole Levi for shooting him. Levi could have captured him and not killed him. I wanted to kill Levi after he did that, but I didn't. Now I think I damn well should have.

"Now he thinks I visited those Russians. Well, Louisa, I damn well did. Tommie did some work for them when they built that place and I went to see them just the other day. I liked what I saw there, and they wanted to help me. So, there I was about to get paid a lot of money from them when that fucking Levi screwed that up." Sue Ann took out more tissues and wiped away more tears.

Louisa moved in even closer. "Sue Ann, do you know exactly what they're doing there?"

She smiled before she replied, "I sure do. They have seven of the most beautiful women in the world there who are here to fuck some political assholes from Washington. The girls told me when I visited that one dickhead from Washington was already there.

"I'm not the smartest person in the world, but I have a notion as to what they're up to. I believe they plan to blackmail those assholes and get them to do what they want them to do in Washington. Louisa, I'm not joking when I say that these women are beautiful. But what struck me was that, while they look like they are twenty-one or something like that, I bet they're no more than sixteen years old.

"While I was there, I made love to Inga, and it was the most beautiful moment of my life. Now what's going to happen to me? I'll be convicted and thrown in jail with all those whores and sluts. Is that what I have to look forward to, Louisa? Tell me—you're a smart woman. You know damn well that I'll be convicted and some asshole judge up here in Carroll County will throw away the key. Hell, I'm a deputy sheriff who betrayed every-one. I don't stand a chance, do I?"

Louisa held Sue Ann's hands again. "Sue Ann, I know that you are well liked, and that makes a dif-ference. I know that this is a serious matter, but you never know how things will turn out. Plus, you are a young woman who will have a life after your debt to society is paid.

"I know this is a terrible time for you to try and think positive. But, Sue Ann, this is not the end of the world for you. It is important that you cooperate with us on all of this. That is always taken into consideration at the end of the day."

Sue Ann looked away. "Louisa, my life is over. I real-ly don't have anything to live for. Nothing you say can change that."

Louisa was about to say something when Sue Ann looked at her. "Can you get me some water please."

Louisa stood. "Of course I can." She turned and walked out of the interrogation room. She didn't see Levi until she walked over to the sheriff's office. He was sitting with the sheriff and Quinn, watching the monitor.

All three looked at her when she walked into the room. Levi was the first to speak. "While I was watching you, I had a crazy idea. Do y'all think we can turn her to work for us to spy on the Russians?"

Louisa responded, "That is far-fetched, Levi. First of all, we couldn't trust her. She might ask them for a whole lot of money, and then what are we dealing with?"

Quinn was still watching Sue Ann on the monitor. He jumped to his feet and screamed, "She has a gun!"

All eyes focused on Sue Ann as she faced the camera and rose one hand holding a note she had just scribbled that read, "FUCK YOU, LEVI!" The other hand pulled the trigger of the pistol she was holding in her mouth. The camera captured the bullet coming out the back of her head. *She slumped to the floor.*

———

YURI DOBROW WAS WATCHING ALE SCHUMER ON THE screen. He saw him leave the bed and take a phone call. That bothered Yuri, as it was totally unexpected. He wondered what Schumer would do after the call. He didn't have to wait long.

Schumer looked at Elena, who was sitting on the bed watching him. "Listen, sweetie, I need to see Yuri—right now."

Elena nodded and left the room. At the same moment, Yuri left his office and headed in that direction. He passed Elena as he opened the door and entered.

Schumer jumped off the bed. "Listen here, I need to leave here immediately. I damn well know what you are up to, and I will have no part of it. You had better get that helicopter of yours fired up and bring me back to Washington, and you had better make it fast!"

Yuri held up both hands. "Senator, just cool down a bit. We will be happy to get you back to Washington, but it will take a few hours, as there is some work being done on our helicopter."

"The sooner the better because the president of the United States knows I'm here. One call from me, and he'll send one of our own Marine choppers to get me! Do you understand?"

"I do, Senator. Please come with me, and we will make you comfortable until the helicopter is ready."

Schumer followed Yuri out of the room and through a long corridor where he opened a door and showed Schumer in. Ale looked around the room and saw paintings on the wall and an area on the far wall that had food trays and beverages.

"Relax, Senator, and I will be back momentarily with news on the progress with the helicopter."

Before Ale could reply, Yuri left the room.

He walked quickly to his office, where his chief of security, Anotoly Kristoff, was waiting. Before he could sit down, Kristoff spoke, "Yuri, I jammed his phone so he cannot make or receive calls.

"My assistant who is monitoring the Carroll County sheriff's radio calls just informed me that an ambulance was dispatched to the sheriff's office. It seems that a female deputy was shot and is in critical condition. I know there is only one female deputy in the department, and it is our new friend, Sue Ann."

Yuri sat behind his desk. "I might suggest that if Sue Ann was shot while at the sheriff's department, that cannot be good for us. My guess is that she gave us up and somehow was shot in the process. That is complicated by the fact that the president of the United States knows that Schumer is here.

"So, my friend, it appears that our operation has ended. It's time to set our evacuation plans in motion. Have your men destroy all the items they need to take care of. We will leave in two hours."

Anatoly looked at him "What of the girls and the senator?"

Yuri smiled. "Bring the girls to the room Schumer is in, and lock them all inside. They will be taken care of when we set off the explosions as we leave."

Anatoly smiled as he left the room.

Yuri sat back in his chair and thought, *Screw you, Senator!*

———

LEVI WAS THE FIRST TO RUSH INTO THE INTERROGATION room. Sue Ann's blood covered the table and chairs. The sheriff had called for an ambulance the moment after he saw her pull the trigger.

Quinn and Louisa looked at each other in shock.

Levi went to her limp body and held her neck. He could not detect a pulse.

Leroy stood in disbelief. "Where in the hell did she get the gun?"

Levi looked down and pulled up the bottom of her trousers. They all saw the ankle holster that she kept her small pistol in. Levi pounded the table. "Jesus Christ, how did I miss that? I'm a fucking idiot! I missed it!"

Within five minutes, the ambulance arrived, and the two paramedics ran up to the sheriff's office. They rushed into the interrogation room and examined Sue Ann. Both looked at each other and advised the sheriff that she was dead.

The sheriff sat back in one of the chairs and fought back tears. "By the love of God, this should have never happened. This is insane!"

The paramedics loaded Sue Ann's body on the stretcher and left without saying a word.

Louisa walked over to talk to Leroy, but she stopped when her phone rang. It was Sandy Winston's name on the screen. She turned and walked out of the room. She hit the answer button. "Hello, Sandy, I hope you have good news for me because I'm presently knee-deep in crap."

"I wish I did, Louisa, but I don't. It seems that that our Russian friends have none other than Senator Schumer at their compound. The president has asked me to fly out on out in our helicopter to get him. I know you are a lot closer than I am, so could you get over there with the county sheriff officers to see what's going on? I should be there within a half hour."

Louisa thought for a second or two. "Okay, Sandy, I can take some officers out there to check it out, but listen, get here as quickly as you can!"

She hung up as she went back into the interrogation room. She looked at Quinn and the sheriff. "I just got off the phone with Sandy Winston. It appears that the Russians have Senator Ale Schumer at the compound. He's flying out in the bureau helicopter and asked if we could go there right now."

Levi perked up and looked at the sheriff. "Listen, Leroy, I need a change of scenery right now. I will take some of our men and head on out there with Louisa and Quinn."

The sheriff looked at Louisa, who nodded in the affirmative.

"Okay, Levi, but all of you be careful because that could get dangerous—and get that way quickly."

Levi stood and looked at Quinn and Louisa. "Let's get some bulletproof vests for you both and be on our way."

Ten minutes later, Quinn and Louisa were in his truck following the two sheriff's patrol cars in front of them, with Levi in the first car. They turned off the Blue Ridge Parkway and headed down Pipers Gap Road.

Within five minutes, they stopped some one hundred yards in front of the compound. Quinn and Louisa got out of his truck and joined Levi with the other five deputies.

Levi looked at them. "These sons of bitches are dangerous assholes. They killed those two in the cabin, and they would like to kill us. So, we gotta be careful!"

No sooner had he said that when they saw some movement from inside the main gate. Bullets started to fly in their direction. The deputies retuned fire with their AR-15s.

Quinn and Louisa were huddled behind his truck. He looked at her. "Did I tell you how stylish *you are in the vest?*"

———————

YURI FINISHED PACKING HIS SATCHEL AND LOOKED AT Anatoly. "It's time to go, my friend." He followed Anatoly through several corridors until they got to the large garage where the helicopter was waiting. Several of his men had already climbed aboard.

Yuri looked at the remote control he was holding. He pushed the three buttons on the control. He looked at Anatoly. "We have three minutes." They climbed aboard and shut the door.

The pilot nodded and pushed a button. The roof started to open, and the side walls collapsed. Within a minute, they were starting their ascent. Once they had cleared the garage, the first explosion happened. The complete front gate complex exploded.

Louisa caught sight of the white helicopter with the cross starting to gain altitude. She reached for her cell phone and punched in a number. In a moment, she heard Sandy Winston answer. "Jesus, Sandy, where are you? They are on their helicopter and are getting away!"

"Oh no they won't, Louisa," was what she heard.

The white helicopter zeroed in on the deputies below and machine gun fire hailed down on them. Quinn and Louisa dove for cover. Their attention was soon taken by the sight of two helicopters hovering some one hundred yards from the white helicopter.

Louisa looked at Quinn. "I recognize the bureau's helicopter, and Sandy must be in that one. But what's the second one?"

Quinn smiled. "That, my dearest, is an AH-64E Apache Guardian!"

The pilot of the white helicopter turned to face the other two. Machine gun fire was now directed toward the two helicopters. The pilot of the Apache Guardian pushed a button, and one Hellfire missile was fired. Within a moment, the white helicopter exploded in midair.

While Levi and the others watched the helicopters above, buildings continued to explode on the compound.

Levi looked at Quinn. "Come with me."

They both ran around the perimeter fence, which led to the rear of the compound.

Once they reached the last building, Levi moved through the door that was partially open. He motioned to Quinn. "I can hear screaming in there."

They both wedged themselves into the building and ran to the room where they thought they heard the screams. They also heard the explosions getting closer. Levi tried to open the door, but it was locked. He pointed his rifle at the lock and fired. The door shattered and fell open. They rushed in to find Senator Schumer and the seven girls huddled behind a sofa.

Levi looked at them. "Follow us now because this building is about to blow!"

They followed Levi out, with Quinn taking up the rear. They all ran as fast as they could until they reached the fence line. Just as they did, the building they'd been in exploded.

Once the debris had settled, they followed Levi to the front of the compound. By then, Virginia State Police officers were on the scene as well as the fire trucks. They could see where the two helicopters had landed.

Louisa and Sandy Winston were waiting for them. Ale Schumer recognized Winston and embraced him. "Jesus, I am glad to see you. I thought I was a dead man!" He looked at Louisa. "Have we met? You look familiar."

She looked at him. "A long time ago, Senator, a long time ago."

He then looked at Quinn and Levi. "And who the hell are you two? You just saved our lives!"

Quinn looked at him. "Senator, this is Levi Blackburn, and he is the senior detective with the Carroll County Sheriff's Department."

The senator embraced Levi. "You are a hero, son, and I'm going to tell the world that you are!"

Winston interrupted, "Senator, it's time for us to leave and get you back to Washington before the press arrives."

Schumer nodded in agreement and headed to the helicopter. Within five minutes, both helicopters took off and headed toward Washington.

Louisa looked at Levi. "Levi Blackburn, *you are a hero!*"

CHAPTER 18

A MONTH HAD PASSED SINCE THE MYSTERIOUS EXPLO-
sion at the church compound in Pipers Gap. The local
and regional press searched for answers as to what had
actually happened there. But no one seemed to know.

The death of Sue Ann Kollman was ruled accidental.
Her funeral was a relatively small affair attended by family and friends. The four people who knew the truth had
a secret to keep for the rest of their lives.

The sheriff still had nightmares of her death. His
wife, Laneisha, was doing her best to convince him to
retire.

Levi was recognized as a hero for saving the seven
beautiful young woman who worked at the compound.
They all left Carroll County in the custody of the
Homeland Security Department.

The president of the United States expelled the Russian ambassador. No retaliatory action was taken on the part of the Russians.

QUINN AND LOUISA FINISHED SUPPER AND KNEW IT WAS time for the hot tub. Quinn opened a special bottle of Michael & David Gluttony zinfandel. He came out on the deck with the bottle and glasses in hand.

Louisa slipped off her robe and sat on the edge of the tub. Quinn filled her glass and gave it to her along with a kiss. Once he filled his glass, he sat beside her on the side of the tub.

He was the first to speak. "So, a month has passed, and our life is sort of back to normal. I don't think I can take much more excitement. All of that was crazy!"

Louisa looked at him. "We just need to tell Leroy that we're out of commission. Done. Finished with police business. You know we have to tell him."

With that, Quinn took another sip of wine and slipped into the tub. Louisa finished her wine and slipped in beside him. They kissed for the longest time until Quinn reached outside of the tub and picked something up.

Louisa looked at him. "What have you got there?" Quinn set a little rubber duck afloat in the tub. Louisa laughed. "Oh, how sweet. Is that for me?" She picked it up and shook it a bit. "There's something in it."

"Open it," Quinn offered.

Louisa carefully separated the duck in half and froze. She reached in with two fingers and careful took out a diamond ring. Quinn took it and placed it on her finger.

"Louisa Hawke, I love you more than anything on this earth. We have been through hell together, and I really should have done this a long time ago. Will you marry me?"

Louisa started to cry and threw her arms around him. "It's about darn time you get around to this, and yes, I will marry you, Quinn McSpain!"

AUTHOR'S NOTE

MOST OF YOU HAVE PROBABLY NEVER HEARD OF POLYCY-
themia vera. It is a slow-growing blood cancer in which
your bone marrow makes too many red blood cells.
These excess cells thicken your blood, slowing its flow.
They also cause complications, such as blood clots,
which can lead to a heart attack or stroke.

Common symptoms of polycythemia vera (PV)
include:
- Tiredness (fatigue)–Itching (especially after a
  warm shower)
- Headache–Sweating (at night or during the day)
- Blurred vision or blind spots–Painful burning or
  numbness of the hands or feet
- Bleeding from the gums and heavy bleeding
  from small cuts–Bone pain

- Shortness of breath–Abdominal pain or discomfort
- Early feeling of fullness when eating–Pain under the left ribs
- Problems concentrating–Dizziness, vertigo, lightheadedness
- Insomnia–Reddening of the face, or a burning feeling on the skin
- Angina (chest pain)–Ringing in the ears

This PV is a rare disease. Approximately 200,000 people in the United States are living with PV. It can occur at any age, but it is more common in people over 60 years of age. It affects slightly more men than women. The cause of PV is unknown and at this point in time and there is no cure.

Is very important that if you think you might have any of the symptoms, you should bring them to the attention of your healthcare provider. There are specific drugs that can keep PV under control.

I know because I have polycythemia vera.

CDG